REALITY

~~bytes~~

'BITES'

a not so innocent love story!

REALITY

~~bytes~~

'BITES'

a not so innocent love story!

Anurag Anand

Srishti
PUBLISHERS & DISTRIBUTORS

SRISHTI PUBLISHERS & DISTRIBUTORS
N-16, C. R. Park
New Delhi 110 019
srishtipublishers@gmail.com

First published by Srishti Publishers & Distributors in 2011

2nd impression, 2011

Typeset in AGaramond 11pt. by Suresh Kumar Sharma at Srishti

Printed and bound in India

Dedicated to:

Neeru – my loving wife and my harshest critic.

Acknowledgements

Behind every story is a figment of reality. In this case, the figment happens to be one of the most cherished and memorable ones from my life – my formative years at the school hostel. This one goes out to all of you who constitute memories so treasured that even the most painful ones make me wish to fly back in time even if it were to be as a mere spectator.

Mr. Rawat, his unfaltering zest to make a sportsman out of everything on two feet and his oft-faltering vocabulary (How can I ever forget the, 'both of you three come here'?); Mr. Kansal, Mr. Bahadur, Mrs. Das, Mrs. Chaudhary and their relentless efforts to bring about a remote resemblance between us and what they would call, 'normal kids'; Baba, Ram Teerath and the extra servings of sweet dish or other rationed delicacies (read – the only edible items served in the hostel mess) that they would lovingly slip on to our plates, our subject teachers – Mrs. Shubhra Malhotra, Mrs. Usha Kaul, Mr. U. S. Arora and all the others whose plight in trying to make scholars out of us, I now understand. Whether you ever read this or not, thank you for all the fond memories.

All the pretty girls in class that knowingly or unknowingly I would have made a pass at (I do remember most of your names but shall refrain from mentioning them here for the sake of harmony in your new found settings); my friends from the hostel (please don't sue me if you find a character in the story adorning your name and mannerisms) and those day scholars whose tiffin boxes I have had the privilege of polishing off (Now you know – it wasn't your mother who packed empty boxes for you all those days); I miss you all.

The list would be incomplete without a mention of Srishti , my publisher, whose efforts beyond the call of business have provided a platform to numerous aspiring authors for telling their stories. And most importantly I would like to thank you, my readers, for your appreciative e-mails and comments that you have made the efforts to share. Clichéd as it may sound, but it is indeed your affection that keeps me going and provides me with the impetus to write. I hope that this book too lives up to your expectations and as always, I shall eagerly await your precious feedback.

Reviews of Anurag Anand's, 'The Quest for Nothing'

The author Anurag Anand manages to retain the reader's interest in the written word throughout the story. It promises to keep your brain cells working, long after you keep the book down... The high point is the book keeps you hooked because of its utter simplicity. Its one that most people would relate to and the contemporary setting makes it more so. And as you stream through the pages, you are bound to sit up more than once and exclaim, 'Hey, that's exactly how it happens with me!'

—Hindustan Times

He (Anurag) infuses intrigue and complexity into a world he is familiar with...

—DNA

The Quest for Nothing is an emotional thriller set in the corporate world. The story looks at the inherent conflict between the career and personal ambitions between individuals.

—The Times of India

... give us a ringside view of corporate conniving, show us how the bad boys in advertising, FMCG and banks are slain... the author does manage to mirror the life of an ambitious, upwardly mobile couple honestly, giving his characters enough flesh to make them credible.

—Hi! Living Magazine

It is a contemporary saga of treachery, deceit and ruthless ambition that explores the fundamentals of human relationships and love.

—The Tribune

The gripping climax deftly uses contemporary mediums like social networking, which makes it highly relatable.

—Indianbookreviews.com

... this book is very special because it deals with the one thing that defines our lives; which is ambition..... Read it, and i am sure you will enjoy it.

—Pritish Nandy

Poet, Filmmaker & Journalist

I was surprised at how quick a read it was, and I was surprised at why i hadn't finished it earlier..... All of us, who are children of middle class India, will find a lot that we can relate to in this book.

—Gul Panag

Film Actor

The most wonderful part of 'The Quest for Nothing' is that it is not set in a fantasy land. It is set in a world that you and I can completely relate to.... I have lived every one of these days that the protagonist lives at least in the first half of the book and for that, for me it was a fantastic read.... It's got romance, it's got drama, it's got relationships... It is full *Paisa Vasool.*

—Mini Mathur

TV & Media Personality

One

10, 9, 8... the countdown had begun. The control room was swarming with people, some of them unknown and yet exuding an aura of importance which betrayed their allegiance to the murky world of politics. As I monitored the complex set of numbers flashing on the control panel, I could see reporters pushing their adversaries and speaking incoherently into their hand-held microphones which bore the insignia of one news channel or the other. The launch of India's first geostationary satellite was an occasion that warranted such enthusiasm. 6, 5, 4... and suddenly as if the world came crashing down. A shrilling noise that would have put fighter jets to shame emanated from all directions, creating a near stampede in the control room.

I tried to press the big red button on the control panel which had the letters, 'ABORT' neatly engraved on it, but I seemed to have lost all control over my hands. I tried and tried again, my hand grazing past the red button to land elsewhere on the panel until I finally hit the bull's eye. The noise instantly ceded and that was when I opened my eyes. I was on my bed in the flat in *Mukherjee Nagar* which had been my home for over three months now. The alarm clock, which now lay toppled on the bed-side stool, had done its job and I was wide awake to face one of the most important days of my life – my first day at the engineering college.

No, I was not going to IIT and No, I was not going to become a Mechanical or an Electronics engineer, streams that my father had selected for me long before I could spell the word 'engineer'. I had only managed a seat in Civil Engineering and that too, just about. If you are thinking that I must be devastated at this ruthless pruning of my ambitions, you couldn't be more wrong. I was elated to have managed all that I did, given the transformation I underwent over the last two years of my life – a metamorphosis that shall unfold as you read on. And yes, thank god for small mercies, for sparing me the horror of enlisting in one of the IITs and eventually landing up in some assembly line or an MBA institute or worse still, writing a book about my supposedly sublime experiences.

First I glanced at the wall clock – 6.30 a.m., before turning towards the rhythmic purring that was now a part and parcel of our lives. Santosh was lying face down on his bed, the pillow covering his head and acting as a silencer for his incessant snoring. The third bed in the room was empty and I guessed that Anirban, after placing the silencer in its place had proceeded to the loo for his marathon early morning session. I drank a glass of water and made my way to the firmly closed toilet door.

"Bengali! Come out. Read rest of the newspaper later, I need to go in there urgently," I yelled, addressing him by the name that had been fondly bestowed upon him in the school hostel.

A name deprived of creativity like most others in this city. For instance, I had just graduated from a school called, 'Delhi High School' – prefix the name of the city to the type of school it was and voila, you have your name. And if you thought that was the end of it, I was now going to attend a college that was called, 'Delhi College of Engineering' – beat that if you can. Had it not been for the names borrowed from the British and numerous indigenous Politicos, sometimes I wonder as to how this city would go about naming its streets.

"Two minutes, I am done," he replied.

It took three reminders with repeated banging of the door and approximately ten more minutes before he decided to concede his throne. I had been thinking about this day for months now and the last thing I wanted was to be late today. So, in all of 20 minutes I was at the *Mukherjee Nagar* bus stop, waiting for the bus to *Kashmiri Gate*. I was wearing my new denims and shirt that I had bought only last week and had successfully managed to conceal from my flat mates for this momentous occasion.

Those of you who have attempted to brave the public transport system in Delhi would know that such a thing called 'time table' does not exist here. So, when you are waiting for a particular bus at the bus stop, you can only pray for it to appear soon or fall prey to the carnivorous species called *Auto Wallas.* But the Gods were kind to me and within ten minutes I saw the bus swiveling towards the waiting passengers. As the conductor banged his hand on the metallic body of the bus, blurting out the names of the stops it was expected to make, a herd of humans converged on the back entrance, pushing and struggling to get on. All I could remember was walking towards the gate and the next thing I knew, I was on the bus, sandwiched between human flesh, bones and god knows what other parts of the anatomy. *I hope I manage to get a seat in the hostel. This is sacrilege.*

The college had limited seats at the in-campus hostel and the allotment was on the basis of the entrance examination rankings – the same logic that was used to decide the stream of engineering one could pursue. I obviously was on the waiting list and hence had to contend with the 'cattle class' journey from *Mukherjee Nagar* to college.

It would have been futile to suggest shifting to a place closer to my college since both my flat mates were pursuing their degrees from colleges in the North Campus of the Delhi University which was a hop, skip and jump away from our flat. As you would have gathered, the three of us were together in the school hostel. Once we were done with our class XIIth boards, we had decided to take up a place together to make it easier for us to submit our college admission forms. And when we returned to Delhi just before our results were declared, it took us all of two days to zero in on this flat.

Well, it wasn't exactly what you would call a flat – it comprised of a room (large enough to house three beds) with built-in cupboards and a bathroom, located on the terrace of a residential building. A separate entrance and the low rent made it a perfect place for three bachelors about to start their college life.

The choice wasn't incorrect since it was extremely convenient to travel together and fill up forms for different subjects in various colleges, most of which were in the vicinity. Due to its proximity to the University Campus, the colony was infested with students to the extent that they comfortably outnumbered the families settled in the area. This had its own set of advantages in the form of hang out joints for students, a society that willingly or unwillingly had got accustomed to late night house parties and the numerous budget eateries that catered to the usually 'broke' student fraternity, at times even extending credit to their regular customers.

Long before the colleges came out with their admission lists, Santosh (aka Senti) had decided that he was going to pursue a B.A. Pass course from the first college that decided to take him and utilize the next three years to prepare for the Civil Services Examination – a near epidemical fetish that seems to breed in the waters of the state he comes from. Bengali ... oops Anirban on the other hand had to wait till the second cut-off list before he enrolled for the English Honors course in *Hansraj College.* I was waiting for the third list so as to manage an admission in Economics at any of the mention worthy colleges when DCE (Delhi College of Engineering) came out with its results.

I am not exactly known for my optimism and wouldn't even have bothered to check the DCE results, had it not been for *her* call. *She* had called me to share the good news that *she* would be joining the Computer Engineering course at DCE and after I had congratulated her, she asked, "What do you think? With your rank, you should manage a seat by the third cut-off too... no?"

I was clueless about what she was talking until I checked the results online. My rank was only 32 ranks below the last candidate to be selected as per the first cut-off list. If luck decided to turn my way, 32 or more students who were ahead of me would prefer a different college or a different course in a different college and not take admission in DCE, paving the way for me to fulfill my father's long cherished dream of having an engineer for a son.

The day the second cut-off list was to be declared, I went to the nearest cyber café, crossing the index and middle fingers of my left hand, from the time I entered till the time I checked the results. I had made it by a whisker and was eligible to join the Civil Engineering course, a situation that could further improve with the third list. The third list never came and here I was, on a DTC Bus (Delhi Transport Corporation – another ingenious name) perspiring my way to the college.

As I walked from the bus stop towards the college, I was engulfed by a familiar sensation of anxiety and fear of the unknown. There were parked cars with parents escorting their offsprings' towards the mammoth gate of the institution. There were groups of students laughing and chatting as they walked past the gate – possibly seniors who were returning to the campus after an end-semester break and then there was me, a solitary soldier taking measured steps towards his goal, burdened with the enormity of the occasion. I paused to look at the gate which had large metallic letters spelling the name of the institution; I could feel a cold bead of sweat trickle down my spine.

I was nervous and I was unsure, a feeling that comes with the unfamiliarity of the territory – a feeling similar to what Lord Rama would have felt during the first days of his exile or that of a foreign tourist when hounded by the *Pandas* on the banks of the holy river *Ganges* in *Benaras.* Soaking in the atmosphere and not attempting to interfere with it, I quietly walked towards the room marked as 'Registrations' and joined the queue of students which was spilling out of the reception area. There were three desks consecutively engaged in registering the newcomers and within minutes I was facing an unfriendly looking fellow with a receding hairline slumped lazily on a chair behind one of the desks.

"Roll Number?" he enquired, extending his hand for a piece of paper that I was now frantically searching for in my file. His annoyance was disturbing. "Atul… Atul Singh, Roll Number 5378917..," I said, as the elusive admission ticket finally presented itself in my view. I quickly pulled it out and placed it in the extended hand. I was made to sign three different documents and given a docket that contained my class schedule, the rules governing life at DCE, the syllabus and a host of other such documents.

"The induction program will start tomorrow at 9.00 in the auditorium, don't be late," he said in a rehearsed manner, shifting his gaze towards the boy behind me, leaving no scope for me to ask any questions. I walked out of the room as quietly as I had entered.

As I walked out of the reception area, my eyes peering into the crowd, I was hoping to find just one familiar face. 'If not her, anyone would do. I am already feeling lost here,' I almost murmured. I had told her about my luck with the results and that we would be attending college together. She seemed happy and excited. "Great. I will see you on the 11th then," she had said. *It is 11th alright and almost 10.00 o'clock now. Where on earth is she?*

I was contemplating pulling out my Mobile Phone and calling *her* when an unknown voice broke my chain of thoughts. "Hey you,"

I heard someone call out from behind me.

I turned around to face a petite boy who seemed my age. "First year?" he quizzed, with a menacing look that was a stark contrast to his personality, but was enough to set the record straight that we were anything but equals. I nodded.

"What...," he said imitating my nod. "Don't you have a bloody tongue? Or don't you know how to speak to your seniors? Say, 'Yes Sir'."

"Yes Sir," I obliged. "Now stop looking at me like a dickhead. You are required in the canteen right away. Walk straight down and turn right between the two buildings and you will find it. The entrance has 'Canteen' written on it. Got it?"

"Yes Sir," I added, walking towards the canteen. *Another stroke of genius! Who could have ever thought of marking the canteen as 'Canteen'? And if the bugger had not told me, I was intending to walk into a room marked as 'Ladies Room' instead... huh!!* I shrugged and smiled to myself as I took the right turn between the two buildings. Indeed the canteen was there, well marked, as I had already been appraised.

I walked in to a big hall with a series of food counters connecting it to what seemed like the kitchen. There were arbitrarily placed rectangular tables on one side, possibly discards from the other half which was now devoid of furniture and had a group of scared students standing in stiff attention. They were facing another group that was comfortably seated in front of them.

"First year?" I heard the same question again, this time from one of the seated beings. "Yes Sir," I replied. "Come, join the gang," he said signaling towards the group that was standing.

Ragging! Let's see what you guys have in store. Only if you knew where I had come from! I glanced at the group, of which I was now a part. It comprised of about 15 students, all males and most of them virtually trembling from the waist down. The scene could have been straight out of a Hollywood film with a group of Jews lined up in front of the Nazi firing squad, awaiting the inevitable. I glanced at my peers again; they looked like the front benchers from school – those with well greased hair, lunch boxes in their bags and bespectacled eyes, exhausted after years of timely submission of homework assignments. *Only if they had stayed in the Delhi High School hostel for a few months, they wouldn't be shitting in their pants right now.*

The feminist brigade seemed to have left its mark on the age old phenomena of ragging as well. While the boys walking into the canteen either joined those on the chairs or were made to stand with us, the girls were pretty much left alone. So while most of the senior girls had joined their class mates, I could see a group of girls standing in one corner, witnessing the proceedings with a strange mix of expressions – pity, relief and amusement.

"Now all of you introduce yourselves one by one. And every sentence you speak needs to start and end with 'kick my butt'. Got it?" one of the seniors barked.

"If you miss out on the 'kick my butts', you will actually get one kick for every miss," another one added with a sense of pride in the ingenious variation he had introduced.

So the introductions began. "Kick-my-butt I am Rohit Gupta kick-my-butt," and so on. While some people went about the task confidently, majority of the orators were still trembling with fear and the words were escaping their mouths with nervous stutters. The seniors were cracking up with laughter, finding some hidden humor in the entire act.

Soon it was my turn and as I began, "Kick-my-butt I am Atul Singh kick-my-butt," I saw a familiar face walk into the canteen. *She* was looking straight into my eyes and smiling as *she* walked towards the group of girls in the corner. There are times when you hope that mother earth would come to your rescue, creating a fissure to swallow you within. This was one of those moments. I was embarrassed and I had no clue as to what I was speaking, fully aware that *she* was witnessing every move I made and could hear every word I spoke.

I focused my vision on the ground in front of me and continued, "Kiss-my-arse, I come from *Hissar* in Haryana and have joined the Civil Engineering course, kiss-my-arse." *What timing! Only if she had walked in a few minutes later, I would have been done and over with this crap.*

"That is 2 kicks," shouted the senior who had suggested the 'kick for a miss' variation, elated at having someone fall into his trap.

"Kicks! But why?" I enquired, "I had added both, the prefix and the suffix."

"And you don't think there is any difference between someone kicking your butt and kissing it?" he replied as I realized my colossal error.

The crowd was in splits and since I was literally the butt of the joke, I continued to miss the humor. *Distractions and how! You can completely count on these girls to distract you from the simplest of tasks and land you in a soup.* I glanced in *her* direction and *she* was still looking straight at me with a smile. Only the smile had widened a bit.

I was short of options. I could either deny them the privilege of watching my butt imitate a soccer ball and create a scene or I could simply give in, swallowing my pride, dignity, self esteem and the likes. The decision had to be quick since the senior in question was already taking his stance – a player waiting for the referee's whistle to take a penalty stroke. The stadium had gone quiet in anticipation and I continued to face him, hiding the object of utmost importance - his soccer ball, from his view.

A few minutes earlier, you could have kicked me all that you wanted. But now, with her watching, I would rather have you kiss my arse. And just when I had almost prepared myself to confront him, the bell came to my rescue. This being the first class of the new semester, the seniors were not keen to miss it and all of them grabbed their notebooks and bags and scampered towards the classrooms.

"The kicks are pending," the senior said to me before addressing the rest of us, "and this was just the introduction. There is more to come, so you guys have fun till we meet again." I was glad to have avoided a run up against their intransigence for now and slowly walked towards where *she* was standing.

The other girls around *her* had started to disperse while she stood there clutching a file and a notebook to *her* chest as a mother would hold her newborn. *She* was looking like the perfect Indian girl, dressed in a light pink *Lucknawi* suit, a complete transformation from what I had last seen of *her*. *Her* hair was neatly pulled back and held together by a pink band and the absence of make-up sans the slight touch of lip gloss made *her* look heavenly.

"So Mr. Kiss-my-arse, how have you been?" *she* said, before bursting into a giddy chuckle. As I struggled to check my complexion from turning into an even darker shade of red, *she* added, "It was hilarious. The look on your face! I couldn't stop laughing."

"I have been good. You tell me? Looking pretty," I said, ignoring any reference to the recent episode and hoping that I had one of those Neutralizers from the movie, 'Men in Black' which could erase all traces of it from *her* memory.

"Thanks. Well, first day of college. You didn't expect me to land up in a skirt, did you? I guess we have the rest of the day off, want to grab a coffee?" *she* asked.

"Sure," I replied, surveying the hall, which looked like it had recently been hit by a tornado, for a table that we could occupy.

"You want to sit here and wait for them to come and give you your pending kicks? Don't be silly. I had seen a *Barista* just a little ahead of the main gate, lets go there," *she* suggested.

She had a point. If the seniors returned while I was still with *her*, the stand-off which had been avoided would be inevitable. Mentally calculating the amount of money required for buying two coffees and maybe a sandwich at *Barista* and the damage it would do to my budgets for rest of the week, I escorted *her* out of the canteen.

"I am glad that you are also here," *she* said, as we walked out of the campus.

I could smell the faint aroma of *her* perfume intermingled with that of *her* body and other cosmetic inventions that *she* would have used. I could feel the warmth of *her* body emanating through the confines of *her* suit, forcing my glands to release a liberal dose of Oxytocin (popularly knows as the love potion), which was slowly but surely taking control of my being. Instinctively I crossed the index and middle fingers of my left hand within the confines of my jeans. I wanted to say much more, but I could only bring myself to respond with a 'me too'.

As we walked towards the coffee shop, I was transported back to the time I had first met *her* - a period, two years back, that had given me so much in life. And the fact that we were together now - was it a part of a larger conspiracy by our respective destinities or yet another cruel coincidence?

TWO

Up until very recently I was totally convinced that sending their children to a hostel was nothing but a way for parents to get back at them for the labor pain, the numerous sleepless nights and a host of other excruciating experiences that they were made to endure in the process of rearing their offsprings. How else can you explain the pride with which they tell every willing ear that their loved one would soon be leaving them and going to a hostel? A sense of achievement which I am sure is similar to that of a butcher when he talks about the healthy goat that he has been raising for slaughter during the *Eid* festivities.

My father, a humble businessman from *Hissar* had settled for his current profession as a compromise when all the engineering colleges in the vicinity had shut their doors to his ambition of becoming an engineer. The origin of this ambition, I would never know, but its obvious implication was that I was to become an engineer and restore some of his damaged pride. I had known this even before I knew what an engineer did for a living and my purpose was continuously reiterated to me, lest I decided to deviate. Being his only child, I had willingly accepted the mantle and like a guided missile, had put myself on course to become an engineer.

I was sent to the nearby English medium school, given tuitions, reference books, two glasses of milk a day and any other conceivable ingredient that went into the making of an engineer.

"You will become a mechanical or an electronics engineer one day and make the entire family proud," he would say, stroking my head. And like an obedient son, I would agree, "yes papa, I will." My grades in school were a testimony to the fact that I was on the right track and every year my father would grin looking at my report card as if he was holding my engineering degree instead.

Life was flowing smoothly till a distant cousin of mine from my mother's side of the family to be precise, managed to get admitted into an engineering college. Suddenly all hell broke loose and my father got into an overdrive. He had been telling everybody that I was going to become an engineer for years now and given that a child from my mother's side of the family had managed it, there was no option left for me but to emulate the feat. If he had his way, he would have gladly made me skip the few years of pending education and hurled me to an engineering college instead.

It was in this vulnerable moment that one of his harebrained associates suggested that I be sent to one of the schools in Delhi that were touted to be factories, successfully producing Doctors and Engineers year after year. So it was decided that I would be going to Delhi to hone myself for the sole objective for which I had descended on earth. Before I knew what hit me, I was on my way to spend two years of my life in the prestigious Delhi High School hostel, hopefully to prepare for my engineering entrance examinations.

The school was spread over a sprawling expanse and was located in the heart of the city. There were separate buildings for the nursery, junior and senior sections and a host of other structures that were later identified as the hostels, the warden quarters and the servant quarters. There were three fully functional swimming pools, four basketball courts and even a squash court – a game that I had not had the privilege of watching even on the television till then. There was an in campus medical center which was bigger than most full fledged hospitals in my home town, a fleet of buses meant to ferry the day scholars (local students who didn't stay in the hostel) and a host of other amenities that a small-town boy like me could only stare at in amazement.

Both my parents had accompanied me to the school and after a brief guided tour by the warden, Mr. Bansal, were now ready to leave me at the mercy of my own fate. "Alok," the warden yelled out at one of the boys passing by, "this is Atul. He has joined the science section of class eleventh. Take him to the third wing, room number 36."

I could see my mother desperately holding back her tears, pursing her lips and looking at me with eyes that did nothing to contain her emotions. I was already reeling under the weight of my own fears and did not have the courage to saddle myself any further. So I quickly bent down, touching my parents feet in one sweeping motion and reached out for my suitcase. Alok had already picked up my other bag and had started walking. I followed him without looking back, fully aware that my parents would not blink an eyelid till I was safely away from the periphery of their vision. I wanted to look back – one last glimpse; I wanted to hug her and ask her to take me back home – I didn't want to stay here, away from them. But I knew that any such action would only make matters worse and so I continued to tread along, my feet seeming like balls of lead.

"So where are you from?" he enquired, jolting the last thread – my thoughts, away from my parents. "I am from *Hissar*, Haryana. You?" I replied.

"First time in a hostel?" he continued his quizzing, ignoring my question. "Yes," I responded, struggling to keep pace with him, the suitcase making the stairs a daunting climb.

My room was on the third floor of one of the three 'wings' of the boys' hostel. It was a small room with two sets of furniture comprising of a bed, a table and a chair. There were two built in wooden cupboards and a side door leading to a small common balcony which had similar doors opening from the other two adjoining rooms.

"It is 5.30," Alok said, looking at his watch. "You have two hours till the dinner bell; you can use this time to set up your bed and the cupboard. Wear your *Kurta Payjama* and come down to the mess once you hear the dinner bell," he continued in a discourse-like fashion.

I had nearly a zillion questions tussling within me to come out, but he didn't seem very conversation prone, so I stuck to the most crucial one, "Who would I be sharing the room with?"

"How on earth would I know!" he snapped with apparent irritation, before checking himself. "The classes start only on Monday and so most people will be joining back only tomorrow (Sunday). Mr. Bansal does the room allocation himself, so you could be sharing it with just about anybody," he added. His irritation now seemed controlled and looking to make the most of this opening, I decided to use the only weapon I could think of. "Care for some *Namak Paree*?" I asked, reaching out for my bag which my mother had stuffed with an assortment of her homemade delicacies.

Though I did not understand the reasons for his annoyance, I knew that if there was one thing that could work as a neutralizer, it had to be a produce from my mother's kitchen. I had seen her tame my father, in his most ferocious of moods, without the use of a single word by simply sliding a plate in front of him.

"I am from *Muzaffarpur*, Bihar," he responded to the question he had earlier ignored, letting words slip out of his mouth amidst the ravenous munching. As the chow took charge of his being, I learnt that Alok was a veteran with his eighth year running in the school hostel and that he was also in the science section of class eleventh. "My room is in the second wing. I shall carry on to change and will catch you for dinner in the mess," he added before stuffing his hands with all the edibles he could – *some for the road.*

I had managed to make my bed and stuff my belongings into one of the cupboards when the chime of the hostel bell announced dinner time. I reached the mess area to be greeted by a sea of unknown faces, all clad in white, some of them looking as lost as me while others surveying the intruders with curious eyes. The mess was a large hall with a human rib-cage like seating arrangement capable of holding and servicing over 400 hungry students at one go. The first two set of rows were reserved for the inmates from the girls hostel while the remaining were available to us on a first come first serve basis. I followed Alok to the corner table of the fourth row and took a seat.

The attendance was far from complete and most of the seats, including the other three on our table remained vacant. I was already feeling like an abandoned tadpole groping to survive in the vast seas and the sight of the watery *Dal* and the excuse for a vegetable that was served to us, only made matters worse.

"Don't worry! In a few days you will get used to the food," Alok remarked, noticing my struggle to swallow the only *chapatti* on my plate.

"Hello Alok! When did you come? How is everything at home?" a melodious voice greeted us as we exited the mess.

I glanced in the direction of the voice to see a girl, wearing the dinner uniform – a white *Salwar Suit*, smiling and walking towards us. "Hi Swati! All well, you tell me," he said with the first smile that I had seen on him all evening. "And this is Atul," he added as an afterthought. "Our class?" she checked with him as she proceeded to shake hands with me. Alok nodded. "Welcome to DHS. I am Swati," she said, before turning back to Alok, "round?"

"Sure," he replied. "After dinner, normally everyone takes a couple of rounds of the school building. It helps in digesting the food. You should come along too," she explained, inviting me to join them. *Digest food? She must be kidding. What food? If I keep eating this food, I would need supplements to survive, let alone exercise to digest it.*

I was in no mood for socializing, but not wanting to antagonize my new class mates, I decided to join. About 80% of the 'round' went in Swati talking about her family and her recent visit home and the remaining 20% went into her quizzing me about my origin and background. After the first round, my obligation was over and I took their leave to return to my room.

"Yaaa… get all the rest you can. Tomorrow, once most of the seniors return, it might get a little more hectic," her parting words were said with a smirk and an ominous undertone that I didn't quite understand.

As I slumped on my bed to spend my first night in the hostel, I realized how lonely life had suddenly become. No, I was not scared of sleeping alone, but I was scared – I was scared of waking up to another day with faces that didn't have a name; I was scared of Alok and his surly demeanor and I was scared of Swati and her talkative nature. I could feel silent drops trickling down from my eyes as my thoughts went back to all that I had left behind – my house, my bed, my parents; and lost in these thoughts I didn't realize when the envelope of sleep finally engulfed me.

I got up early the next morning and as I walked towards the common bathroom, I was glad to have joined the hostel with a day to spare before the classes actually began. This allowed me some time to settle in before the rigmarole of classes and studies and books and tests commenced.

I entered the bathroom and took position behind one of the wash basins to brush my teeth. The three toilets were all locked and of the showers facing them, the only one with an intact door was also taken. Amid the sound of running water, one could hear a song in a language that I couldn't quite comprehend. Soon, the door of the shower opened and the source of the voice – a boy, visibly from the north eastern part of the country emerged. As I looked at his reflection from the mirror in front of me, I got the first of my many shocks for the day. He was stark naked and the towel which could well have been used to conceal his dignity was hanging loose on his shoulders. He walked past me squeezing his underwear with both hands looking as comfortable with his condition as he would have been at the time of his birth.

Once I was done brushing, I went and stood outside one of the toilet doors waiting patiently for my turn. In just a few minutes, a few more boys converged into the bathroom; thankfully all of them covering their private parts with either a wrapped towel or an underwear. A young fellow, who I guessed would be in class sixth or seventh, had just started brushing in front of one of the wash basins when another boy emerged behind him and pulled off his towel.

"Kalu, why are you hiding your little toothpick? Let the world see what you've got," he yelled amidst cheer and laughter from the spectators. Kalu meanwhile showered his tormentor with the choicest of expletives, challenging him to a contest for determining which of the two had been bestowed with a bigger token of manhood.

I watched in utter amazement as both the warring parties held their organs in their hands, stroking them for the benefit of size and measuring them against each other. Though Kalu did not concede till the end, the other boy was visibility better endowed and he expressed his victory by performing a little jig in front of the mirror. His happiness knew no bounds, as if the makers of the *Anaconda* movie had selected his underwear as the location for shooting the next sequel. The war had ended inconclusively but it had fuelled a completely different one within me – one that had pitted the values I had tediously assimilated in my life against the wayward ways of the hostel. Hastily I concluded my other engagements in the bathroom and proceeded to the mess for breakfast.

I looked around for Alok and when I couldn't spot him, I settled for a table that was occupied by two younger looking boys. Apart from a brief round of introductions, the breakfast concluded uneventfully. The breads, eggs, cornflakes and milk did not leave much scope for the chefs to add their own flavor and though the milk was watery and the bread a little harder than usual, I emerged relatively stuffed from the mess. Swati was having an animated discussion with a group of girls near the exit and as I tried to sneak past, she spotted me.

"Hey Atul! Hope you have settled in by now," she enquired. I politely replied in the affirmative, thanked her for the concern and excused myself.

Except for a mouth that went on and on like a car without brakes, she seemed like an ok girl. I did feel a discomforting uneasiness around her, possibly stemming from the deprivation of any meaningful contact with the fairer gender in my past life. In fact I had never been at complete ease even in the company of my female cousins and now when the surroundings demanded a sociable conduct from me, I invariably found myself tongue tied. Even the military provides time to their troops for acclimatization in a new terrain and here I was, expected to communicate with one of the most vociferous samples from the female-kind for my initiation. As I walked away from them I could hear the girls burst out in a giddy laughter, possibly resulting from a joke of which I was the butt. But then, who cared.

I kept wandering around aimlessly, checking out and admiring various sections of the campus and when the heat of the sun became unbearable, I headed back towards the hostel. "Hey you! New admission?" I heard someone call out. I turned around to face a tall, well built man who would have been a misfit in any degree college, let alone a high school. Had it not been for the authoritative tone, I could easily have confused him as a parent who had come to drop his child to the hostel. "Yes," I replied, craning my neck to catch his line of vision. "Here, hold this and follow me," he commanded like an army general, handing me the bag that had been loosely dangling on his shoulder and which seemed to have multiplied manifold in weight as it landed in my arms. When someone built like that commands you to do something in a place that you have just started discovering, the only thing you can bring yourself to do is follow the instructions and so I did.

"Walk fast. Haven't had your breakfast or what?" his words acted as a key to some hidden source of energy within me and despite the bag, I reached the door of his room falling barely a few steps behind. "Hello Lambu Bhaia," I heard one of the juniors wish him on the way, which he acknowledged with a slight nod of the head. *What an apt name!* "Where are you from?" started the usual quizzing as I placed the bag in front of the cupboard in his single room and he parked himself on the bed. "Tiring journey… phew. Do one thing, take off your shoes and walk on my back for a few minutes," he said, spreading himself in a spread-eagle position on the bed. The 'few minutes' lasted over half an hour and the simple act of walking on his back turned into a full fledged body massage. By the time I came out of Lambu's room, it was almost lunch time and I was as tired as a corpse.

The mess was almost full during lunch. The students, a good mix of new admissions and old timers had been arriving since the morning. I looked around and spotted Alok sitting with two other boys on one of the tables. "Can I join you guys?" I checked, interrupting the lively conversation that was underway. "Yaa," he said, before proceeding with a brief round of introductions, "This is Atul, our class. Anirban and he is Bobby." After shaking hands with the other two, I addressed Alok, "I looked for you during breakfast, but couldn't find you." "Yaa, I got up late," he replied curtly before reverting to the conversation that had been interrupted by my arrival. He was describing a scene from some Hollywood movie he had seen during the vacations.

I wanted to know the name of the movie they were discussing and I wanted to tell him about my first morning in the hostel, but he didn't seem interested. The other two asked me the usual questions about my background and before I knew, the lunch was over. The meal was as tasteless as the first one that I had barely eaten in the same mess but somehow I had managed to eat three *chapattis* and some rice as well. *I guess this is what 'getting used to' means.* I declined Anirban's offer for a 'round' and instead headed back to my room. Within minutes of surrendering myself to the bed, I was sound asleep.

My sleep was disturbed with the arrival of my room mate; another scared newcomer looking as lost as a needle in a hay sack. My role was suddenly reversed, it was a welcome change from being the guided to playing the guide. I asked him the same set of questions that I had been showered with since my arrival on the campus. Santosh (a name that was later transformed to Senti) was from *Giridih* in Jharkhand; another engineering aspirant who had been packed away to the unknown land for carving out his destiny. I helped him set his bed and his cupboard, passed on as much information as I had managed to gather and escorted him to the mess for dinner.

Alok was already sitting at a table with no spare seats, so we walked ahead and joined Anirban on a different table. I introduced Santosh to him and in turn he introduced us to the other two diners he was sitting with. Anirban hailed from *Kolkata* and had joined the hostel in class ninth. He seemed much more hospitable than Alok and made us feel at ease, giving us pointers about life in DHS hostel and pointing out key characters as he spotted them on their respective tables.

It was during the conversation with Anirban that I learnt about the prevailing hierarchy within the hostel inmates. Seniority was the first basis of differentiation followed by the number of years spent in the hostel. So, while the word of a senior was next only to that of God, within the same class the boys who had more number of years in the hostel under their belt wielded greater authority. There was a slight grey area between newly admitted seniors and their immediate juniors who were old hands and any confrontations between these segments was settled on a case to case basis, often by the intervention of an old senior who had an unyielding authority over both. This partly explained Alok's cold attitude towards me since like the rigid caste system prevalent outside the boundaries of the hostel, the inmates also preferred to stick around with blokes of their kind and stature.

Then there were the regional sub-groups, the two largest and most volatile ones being those from the state of *Bihar* and the *North East*. There were instances in the past when a harmless confrontation between two individuals belonging to different regions had taken the magnitude of an intra-hostel civil war when others had jumped in to side with the one from their region. However, all the demarcation and divisions within the hostel were erased when it came to facing the common enemy, namely the day scholars. Day scholars, though much larger in number were at the bottom of the schools unwritten pyramid primarily for the lack of any unity. Whereas, in case a hosteller got into a fight with a day scholar, any other hosteller who happened to pass by was sure to jump in without waiting for an explanation about whose fault it was. This sense of 'brother-in-arms' had made the hostel into a power center of sorts.

It was all straight out of a mafia movie and we were listening to Anirban's narration and anecdotes with utter dismay and fascination reserved by children for the bed time stories told by their grand parents. It had all the ingredients of a pot boiler – a clan like hierarchy, unwritten yet all-pervasive rules and a handful of hostellers bound together by the separation from their loved ones, dictating terms against the vast majority of day scholars. Santosh's eyes were on the verge of popping into his plate from their sockets when the discourse was interrupted by the banging of a serving spoon on a large water jug. All eyes shifted to the table in question, where the individual responsible for the sound was now getting up to address the audience.

"That's Brajesh, the Hostel Head Boy," whispered Anirban. "Good evening everybody, I am Braj and I would like to welcome all of you into this new session. I would request all the newcomers from the boy's hostel to proceed to the second wing after dinner. We will assemble at the second floor balcony for an informal round of introductions. Thank you," he said, receding to his seat and leaving the mess buzzing with hundreds of hushed whispers. "Just follow everything that they say and don't answer back, no matter what they ask you to do," our dinner concluded with Anirban's parting words of wisdom.

As we were ambling out of the mess, Swati walked up beside me and said, "Good luck Champ," with a smile that could have signified anything from scorn to genuine sympathy. I decided to give her the benefit of doubt. Santosh was virtually shitting bricks, "What will happen to us? I have heard that they make you pee on live electrical wires in these sessions. God, save me just this one time." I was scared too but could not bear to express it, lest he got a cardiac seizure or something. So, instead I was valiantly trying to calm him down. "Don't worry; they are not going to kill us. Those stories you have heard are terribly exaggerated," I said, putting my arm around his trembling shoulder.

Second wing had been strategically selected for the event since it was located between the other two wings and safely shielded from the outside, especially a curious view from the staff quarters. There were about 8 to 10 seniors talking among themselves; a couple of them having lit up their after dinner smoke, as they waited for the terrified subjects to assemble. After a few other boys joined us, one of the seniors asked us to stand in ascending order of our heights and introduce ourselves. We were taught the famous DHS salute, which mandated us to hold our private parts with one hand and salute with the other, shouting "Hail Seniors" at the top of our voices. Only, this had to be done adorning nothing but our undergarments.

After a few more simple acts comprising of song recitations and dance performances, those in class eighth or below were permitted to disperse, leaving seven of us behind for the grand finale. The finale was an assortment of acts suggested by individual seniors who also identified their favored performers. "Ok. You two," barked one of the seniors, "For two minutes, one of you will act as a boy and the other a girl and you need to seduce each other. The roles will then be reversed and the one who does a better job will be let off for rest of the evening while the other will have to wash my clothes for one full week." Santosh and I stepped forward, not knowing what to do.

"Let this one be. I have something else in mind for him," Lambu spoke for the first time that evening.

"Jaat, you go back for now," he added, signaling one of the others boys to join Senti. Lambu's personality obviously made him a revered entity even among his peers and no one objected to his interference. I did not realize then but I had just been rechristened and my new name was to become my identity for the rest of my stay in the hostel.

Obviously, both the performers had never had the experience of seducing a girl and their antics got the entire group in splits – feeling each other like one would inspect a mango to ascertain its ripeness and moans that could be likened to that of a man on his deathbed. The adversaries were well matched until Santosh's innovation of nibbling the other guy's nipples with a cat-like growl, propelled him to victory and saved him from the week long washing contract.

There was no exaltation in the triumph and I could see his eyes grow moist with indignation, with angry impotence and the pain of having shamed himself. I could completely empathize with him as had it not been for the little twist of fate, I would have been standing there, countering the same set of emotions.

Next, *Lambu* asked me to translate a raunchy Hindi song into *Haryanvi* and dance to its tune. I guess, I would have unknowingly stuck some chord with him during the massage session earlier in the day and he had repaid at a time that I could not depend on any other quarters for help. I proceeded with my act, thanking him from the depth of my heart with every shake of the hip and pelvic thrust that I made. This was a piece of cake compared with what the others had been made to go through and I was relieved.

Later that night, as I resigned to the comfort of my bed thinking about the next day and preparing myself for my first day in class, I could hear Santosh sniffing under his pillow. My heart went out to him and I wanted to walk up and console him, but a part of me knew that our battle had just begun and no amount of sympathy was going to get him to sail through it. So, I went off to sleep, leaving him to conquer his own demons.

Three

When we emerged from the hostel mess, the aluminum glow of dawn was in the process of being consumed by the golden of the radiant morning. Anirban was leading us to the morning assembly, a sea of students clad in white assembled in a military-battalion like fashion in the large field. I felt like a frog from the well who, at the blink of an eye finds himself in a vastness he had never even dreamt of. I wanted to soak in as much as the surroundings had to offer, but my limbs seemed to fail me. I could feel a sweet tinge of pain in muscles whose existence in my body had remained concealed from me over all these years.

Morning P.T. (Physical Training), an intense workout session that lasted for half an hour and seemed like eternity was to blame for my aching existence. The piercing resonance of the hostel bell had dragged us out of bed at some unearthly hour and we had been made to jog, sprint, jump and subject our body to a host of other atrocities in its semi woken state.

"Don't miss the morning P.T. The absentees will be made to go through the same regime in the afternoon heat and only then will they be permitted to have lunch," Anirban's words from the last evening had quashed any sleep induced streak of civil disobedience even before it could surface and here I was, starting my first day of school as flushed as a cockroach in an overflowing sewer.

I dragged myself along for the remainder of the school hours, listening to the introductions of various subject teachers, collecting the syllabus hand-outs, noting down the recommended readings and repeating my own well rehearsed intro for the benefit of every new teacher that made an appearance. In between classes, a bunch of students would round up the newcomers and quiz them on the informal tidbits that had escaped their formal introductions - a merry group of girls and boys entertaining themselves at the cost of the bewildered souls who were still to find their footing in the institution.

This was penny ante stuff in comparison with last nights session in the hostel and somewhere within I was waiting for them to summon me and initiate a conversation – I wanted to be a part of the merry making. I had heard all my classmates repeat their introductions and a few names had managed to stick as well, but if I was to spend the next two years of my life among them, I wanted to know them beyond their names and the number of years they had spent in the school.

The girls were as participative as the boys – talking and laughing and sitting on the desks and giving high fives to each other, I was curious. They were an unknown commodity in their white shirts and skirts that ended a few inches above the kneecap and I felt like a child visiting a zoo for the first time. I wanted to chat with them and observe them and know them better, but my unfamiliarity with the surroundings was restraining and had in turn reduced me into the caged animal that had to wait patiently for the inquisitive child to approach him so as to satisfy his own curiosity.

"Atul, right?" one of the boys walked up to me just when the fourth period ended, announcing the start of the twenty minute break. I nodded.

"From the hostel?" he continued, parking himself on the desk next to mine. As I replied in the affirmative, I could sense a few curious eyes glancing and some unsure strides being taken in our direction. "Atul," I heard Alok yell out, "Come, else we will get late for the snacks." His words had a magical effect and suddenly all the interest that I had aroused among my classmates evaporated. The approaching steps paused before being hurriedly retraced and the gaze of the prying eyes shifted into oblivion. "Cool!! Welcome to DHS. We'll catch up," he said, leaving me to join Alok.

The hostel mess served tea and snacks during the break time while the day scholars feasted on their lunch boxes or the edibles sold in the canteen. "Was he trying to act smart?" Alok enquired, obviously referring to my recently interrupted conversation. "No, no. He was generally talking."

"You don't know these guys. Give them a hand and before you know, they would have mounted you from the rear. And this fellow Manav, he is an arsehole of the highest order. If he acts funny, just sock the son-of-a-bitch in the face," he said with a contempt one normally reserves for his sworn enemies. I did not know then, but I had just been inducted into the age old 'hosteller – day scholar' rivalry that plagued the campus.

The weeks that followed were brimming with revelations and discoveries that were enough to challenge the learned philosophies of life for any sane individual. I learnt that the easiest way to pick up a new language was to start with the swear words and before I even realized, I had transformed into a multi lingual entity, capable of decorating the mother and sisters of any rival in seven different languages ranging from Malayalam to Manipuri.

I realized that a game of cricket can be played within the confines of one of the balconies in the hostel with a hard bound notebook doubling up as a bat. I experienced that despite all the hue and cry about ragging, it was at best a matter of official indifference and the authorities were well aware of all the happenings but preferred to keep themselves at bay unless matters threatened to get out of hand.

Being summoned by a senior to wash his clothes, get him a bottle of water or give him a massage was like lightening and could strike just about anytime and on anyone, irrespective of whether the victim was sleeping or studying or engaged in any other task of vital personal importance. I had also mastered the subtle art of deriving delicious pleasure of vengeance from this servitude by actions that I would only have attributed to a demented soul till the very recent past – actions like dipping washed garments in the lavatory before returning them or spitting in a bottle of drinking water before serving it to a senior who you didn't much appreciate.

Though I had seen some of the juniors dip the garments they were given to wash in the pot, I could not bring myself to engage in the act up until very recently. It was Malay (meaning Monkey in Manipuri), a senior from the north eastern state whose real name I never got to know, who made me first taste the contentment from this manic revenge. Malay had a habit of walking into our rooms at odd hours of the night and giving us truckloads of garments to wash including his dirty underwear and stinking socks. It was one such night when he pulled me from my study table that I decided to give his clothes the 'pot treatment' and the satisfaction that followed almost made me addicted to it. However, the humane side of me which was struggling against being buried in a deep abyss got me to make exceptions for seniors who were not too frequent with delegation of their chores.

The most startling of revelations however came about one Sunday evening when I got up from my afternoon nap. Senti and the chair next to his study table were missing and I safely assumed that he had parked himself in the adjoining balcony to study. The door to the balcony was slightly ajar and I could see him sitting on the chair, holding a thick Chemistry reference book in his hand. The only thing that didn't fit with the picture was that he seemed to be looking away from the book, staring at something at a distance. Puzzled, I craned my neck further from the bed to look at the cause for his distraction and I saw a pretty, smiling face staring back at him from the roof of one of the buildings behind the hostel.

I was amused and shocked at the same time. *Wow. Senti and a girl! An odd combination, but interesting.* In need of a better perspective, I left the bed and stealthily placed myself near the crack in the door, observing the developments. There were none. For the whole of two minutes Senti kept looking at the girl and she kept holding his gaze with the charming smile of a girl wanting to be loved. I had seen enough so I decided to introduce myself into the picture and walked into the balcony, pushing open the door. The girl was the first to see me and instantly turned back and vanished; while Senti shifted his gaze to the book that had been dangling in his hand for god knows how long.

"Oh, you got up?" he turned to me, attempting to negotiate the unexpected intrusion.

The excitement of having discovered the unthinkable was overbearing and had I been in a bath tub, who knows I too could have jumped out in the buff, shouting *'Eureka'* like Archimedes. This was by no means a lesser discovery than buoyancy and my excitement knew no bounds.

"*Kaminey*... I am sure you would want to believe that I am

sleepwalking and did not notice anything. *Sala, chupa rustam,*" I said with a smirk, revealing my newly informed status. "Meaning?" he attempted to shield his guilt behind the garb of ignorance, but to no avail. Soon, he was blurting out the story of his heart, almost relieved at having found a willing and hopefully reliable ear.

He did not know who she was or what she was called. He had first seen her on the same terrace about a couple of weeks back and like any boy our age; he had let his gaze linger along a few moments beyond the casual. Personally I would rate her six on ten but Senti's miasma clad eyes found her to be in a league that was almost sublime. "She is not like the other girls you see; wearing short skirts and all that. She is a girl who knows her roots and yet is prettier than any that I have set my eyes on. Man, you should see her mischievous eyes when she smiles," he sighed, leaving me to compare his verbal portrait with the just-above-average, half concealed in a *dupatta* – face that I had seen.

But my opinions did not matter. What mattered was that there was something so drastic happening right under my nose and I was caught unaware. *Senti in love!! Wow.* I had to know it all and so I persisted with my quizzing, making my blushing roommate spill the safely guarded beans.

The eye lock lasted only for a couple of minutes the first day after which she disappeared, 'stirring him from within' in Senti's own words. He, like a cub who had his first taste of blood, made the balcony his hunting ground, parking himself on a chair every late afternoon with the hope of catching her on the terrace again. And catch her he did. On the third day, she appeared again and gave him the first of her 'lethal' smiles. Needless to say that a fellow from *Giridih*, who had just about landed in Delhi and preferred the company of his books to any breathing life form was as easy a target as could be.

The whole thing was amusing. Senti, a guy you could place your last penny on to recite the entire *periodic table* was suddenly sounding like a character straight out of a romantic novel. "From that day on, she has been coming to the terrace everyday. I think I am in love with her," he said, blinking his eyes like a puppy looking at his master in anticipation of food.

"So, have you spoken to her yet?" I needed all the possible information to come up with a correct diagnosis. "No."

"You mean, for the past 15 days, you guys have just been looking at each other and smiling?"

"Yes." I could have pulled my hair off. The situation was rather grave and unless it got a resurrecting shot in the arm, it had every chance of fizzing out soon. "Well, we need to get you guys talking," I had put my thinking cap on and before long, with the snap of a finger; I announced the emergence of a solution. "Write to her."

"What? You mean a love letter?" he looked at me astonished as if I had just asked him to commit cold-blooded murder. "No. Not a love letter, a simple letter, telling her who you are and asking her to dish out some basic information, like her name." A letter was certainly different from a love letter; the terminology made all the difference and he was soon scanning his desk for the best available stationary. In the absence of a pink glitter pen, we settled for a blue *Reynolds* and put our heads together to come up with his first love letter.

Though I would have liked for it to be more dramatic, Senti was weary lest it transgressed into the territory of being a 'love letter' and hence stuck to the basics, overruling even an exaggerated punctuation mark. In the end, we had a brief introduction of Senti that could well have acted as his makeshift resume, followed by a request to furnish similar information, neatly penned down on a piece of paper. The challenge now was to get it delivered and once again, my ingenuity came to our assistance. We decided to wrap the letter to a stone, which he could hurl towards her when they next met for their eye-to-eye session.

That evening after dinner, we selected a handful of stones that had enough weight to carry the letter to the roof of the next building but were not large enough to inflict grave bodily harm on the recipient if the landing did not go as planned. Senti wrapped the carefully crafted letter on the chosen carrier, flinching as the neat piece of paper crumpled in his hands. The missile was ready and we had to wait till the next day for the target to show up.

Among the zillion definitions of love that I would have come across, none of them warned me of its contagious nature. After carefully placing the enveloped stone in his cupboard, Senti had gone on a discourse about his feelings and emotions till an obscene hour of the night. My fascination and amusement had quickly worn off and not meaning to offend him, I had laboriously listened while he compared his beloved to everything from fairies to flowers and birds to beasts.

Despite the exhaustion of the previous night, I had woken up the next morning with a nervous excitement about how the day would unfold and whether our carefully crafted plans would yield the desired results. It must have been this state of mind that made me see her in a different light for the first time that day. We had been in the same class for over a couple of months now and though she was clearly one of the most cheerful and lively girls in class, it seemed I had ignored her like I had the rest belonging to her gender. 'Ayesha, Ayesha Kapoor', I remembered her Bond'esque introduction which was possibly the only time that we had spoken till date.

As she walked into the classroom, a couple of other girls in tow, she looked like one of the *Bollywood* starlets, flanked by extras who despite being nice-looking often go unnoticed, effortlessly overshadowed by her aura. As she dexterously maneuvered her fragile self, negotiating the rows of desks and benches to reach her seat, I suddenly realized how astonishing she looked. The half sleeved shirt with a few additional folds, baring her beautiful arms; the white skirt that swayed with every step she took and the shapely, marble-sculpture-like legs that emerged from within them; her socks, rolled down to the helm of her shoes; her raven black hair, carelessly tied in a pony, leaving specks to dangle freely on her forehead – she truly looked like a diva amidst a bunch of mortals.

Suddenly, all of Senti's bantering started to make sense. The roses, the lilies, the rabbits and the dove, she had a little of everything in her. Had it not been for worldly compulsions, I would have been happy to sit and stare at her all day, but given the constraints I managed frequent transitory peeks to capture in my eyes as many images of her as I could. Soon the school time was over and we were back to the confines of our hostel room after an excuse for a lunch at the hostel mess. I didn't know whether Senti's experience had made Ayesha into a real and accessible being for me or whether the veil of ignorance had been lifted by an act of god, but I couldn't stop myself from thinking about her.

I was distracted. *She would have reached home by now. She would have eaten her lunch. She would probably be sleeping now, in her house clothes. What would she be wearing? How would she look in her house clothes? I wish I could get to see her in clothes other than the school uniform. She would look stunning in almost about anything.* I had returned to my room physically, but it seemed as if a part of me had boarded the school bus with Ayesha and was now shadowing her, relaying a running commentary to some receiver within my head. I simply could not think beyond her.

"Yaar, all this is too scary. What if she shows the letter to someone or.. or.. gives it to the warden?" Senti was pacing up and down the room in a state of hysteria on steroids.

"Stop being a dickhead, will you? Why on earth will she look at you and smile everyday, only to hand over the letter to the warden? And even if she does so, we haven't written anything untoward in there, have we?" I said, coming back to the moment and pointing my fingers towards our handiwork of the preceding day which was now carefully placed in the center of his study table.

He was a case of jumbled nerves and I had to calm him down somehow. So like *Krishna*, motivating *Arjuna* to slay his own relatives, I gave him a discourse on the futility of everything in life but for true love.

"You know she loves you and now you only need to show her that you are a man and take the first step. Don't think about all that could go wrong, think about all the good things that this might lead to. Girls like their men strong and gutsy, you wouldn't want to come across as a dude with one ball short who couldn't even make the first move, would you?" I went on and on till his expressions changed to that of unshakable resolve. *I will kill him if he decides to back out now.*

When the time came, he took his chair and the Chemistry Book and headed for the balcony while I placed myself behind the slightly ajar door for a ringside view of the happenings. Ten odd minutes of wait and I saw her surface on the roof and take position on the railing to assault Senti with her sparkling smile. Like a revolving radar, Senti surveyed the surroundings before locking his gaze with hers.

"Now! Get up and throw the stone now," I whispered every 30 seconds, increasing my pitch a notch every subsequent time. But Senti was happily returning the smile, oblivious to my existence and deaf to my whispers.

"Ok, if you don't do it now, I am coming out and doing it while you continue to scratch your balls," my words finally caught his attention.

He shifted uneasily in the chair before finally getting up and waving the contents of his hand to her like a cricket umpire showing the ball to both team captains before the start of play. She looked confused and before she could react, Senti hurled the stone towards her. It landed a few meters behind her with a thud. She gave him one last glance before receding, hopefully to pick up the message. We waited for her to resurface for another half an hour before Senti finally decided to call it a day.

"I don't know if she got it or not? She should at least have let me know that she got it. And what if she gets offended or angry and never comes back to the balcony?"

"You have done what you had to, now stop thinking about it. If she gets offended by this and never comes back, there is nothing that you stand to lose. It only means that she was fooling around with you and your relationship would anyways not have gone any further."

That evening, Senti tried to engage me in an exercise of creating various hypothetical scenarios and predicting the possible way forward for his love life. I obliged for a couple of scenarios before excusing myself. I had my own calling to attend to. Ayesha was waiting for me in the world of my thoughts and I had to get back to her.

Four

Life was comfortably tiding along and I didn't realize when the hostel gave up its angry ways and transitioned from the rough unfriendly sea it had been to a much calmer and smoother one. Or maybe, I had simply learnt to negotiate the waters better. The seniors it seemed had taken to washing their own linen and dirtying their hands with other menial tasks and hence the chores relegated to me where now far and few. The juniors, though always courteous, exhibited a certain sense of awe and maybe even fear in their interactions. Alok had overcome his fear of being seen with a newcomer in public and though not exactly the best of friends, we had both found a comfortable pedestal of cordiality, which was a noteworthy progress from the initial days.

I had been instrumental in smuggling a television set and a CD player into the hostel for a night long screening of porn movies. No, it wasn't a brainchild of mine; it had been a regular pastime for the hostel inmates, only I was playing an active role in the arrangements for the first time. For someone who had only depended on select television shows and the odd visit to the neighboring cyber café in *Hissar* for satisfying his primal urges, this was indeed an opportunity of a lifetime. So when one of the seniors entrusted me with the task of collecting money for the adventure, I was thrilled and took up the responsibility with consummate enthusiasm.

I visited each and every room in the third wing, collecting Rs. 10 per head (and settling for whatever I could get from those who exhibited symptoms of a heart condition at the mention of the contribution amount) and comfortably meeting the target of Rs. 450 – standard rental charges for the required equipment after accounting for the 'student discount'.

The tried and tested supply chain managed the delivery through the usual discreet channels and on Friday night the screening was organized in one of the dormitories attended by about 50 people ranging from those in class 6th to class 12th. The junior-most hostel mates (from class 4 and 5) were assigned surveillance duties to sound an alarm if the warden was spotted venturing towards the hostel for one of his infamous inspections. Though they grudgingly took up their assigned posts, I could swear that I saw some of their faces glued on to the TV screen from the dormitory window – like me, getting a taste of their first porn flick.

I had bunked morning P.T. and classes, I had played pranks and been target of pranks – getting up with toothpaste smeared hair and face plastered with shoe polish, taking all of it in my stride. I had tried smoking – cigarettes and weed and *bidis*, and I had tasted cheap whiskey mixed in water from a used *Bisleri* bottle. And then there were those activities that I was not actively involved in but had been a witness to, an equal crime in the eyes of law. Undergarments stolen from the girls' hostel had passed my hands and I had seen them being extracted from their makeshift clothes line on the windows through a contraption created by straightening cloth hangers and mounting them on long sticks. I had seen juniors being made to kneel down for hours for trivial crimes and I had seen locks from cupboards, suspected of concealing edibles, being broken in the absence of their rightful owners.

I had not known then, but all these were unwritten modules of an orientation program and somewhere along the way, my concerted efforts had led to my successful induction into the hostel. The hostel had now embraced me with open arms and vice versa.

While I continued with the rigmarole of hostel life, my emotions graduating from compulsion to intrigue to acceptance to enjoyment, all this while I was carrying a burden on my heart – the burden of love. It was when I was alone, in the confines of my room or otherwise that this burden surfaced in its most magnanimous avatar, bringing with it a sweet tingling pain. I would think about her; I would imagine her near me, with me, under me; I would fantasize, she being the damsel in distress and me the savior, making up situations or borrowing them from some or the other movie that I had seen. I tried to not think about her and I tried to think about other girls instead, but nothing seemed to be working; the burden would just not leave me alone.

Meanwhile Senti had made some remarkable progress in matters pertaining to his heart. The day after we had made the first contact, we heard from her; the medium being the same stone that we had used to transport our message. Only, this time it landed on an unsuspecting Senti's head making us thank our stars for the judicious size selection. He had been sitting at his regular spot, anxiously flipping his Chemistry book when the reply landed on his head. She stayed at her post just long enough to let Senti catch a glimpse of the source before receding into oblivion yet again.

"*Pyare* Santosi *Ji*," the first set of words on the piece of paper almost had me rolling on the floor. The rest of the letter was scrawled in *Hinglish* and after putting our heads together to decipher it, we concluded that it contained an introduction as basic as the one we had laboriously prepared. "Who the fuck is Sharif?" exclaimed Santosh, chuckling at his hideous attempt at imitating a popular song.

Sharif could have been any of numerous administrative and other support staff who stayed in the staff quarters within the campus. She had introduced herself as Zehnab, Sharif's sister. She had recently completed her graduation and had come to Delhi to look for a job.

"And she hasn't even written where she has come from and how long she intends to stay," a fraught Senti was latching on to any pretext for venting his frustrations on the obvious limitations of the medium for the amount of information it could carry.

"What have you got to do with who Sharif is or where she has come from? Can't you see she is some good five years elder to you? Just forget about her and look for someone your age and type," I tried to put into words something that he was anyways struggling to come to terms with.

"I know, but… She doesn't look that old. And she always knew that I was still in school. What then was the point of giving me all those hints?" he was feeling cheated and wronged and rightfully so. There was little I could do for him other than a bit of counseling that I knew was falling on deaf years. The first end-term examinations were just round the corner and I hoped that he would be able to overcome his grief and spend some time actually looking at the books rather than simply holding them like he had been doing for about a month now.

The exams were looming on the periphery and Senti was living the life of a disgruntled lover to the hilt – mostly keeping to himself and snapping at every potential candidate at the slightest of pretexts. My situation was no better. There was a battle waging within me between *Pythagoras* and Ayesha and she, despite her fragile structure was emerging a clear winner.

I had made some progress, if saying 'hi' a couple of times construes for any, but the overall situation was grim. It was easy to rebuke Senti for his inaction in matters pertaining to the heart, but when it came to my own, it was a completely different ball game. I liked to believe that the virtue of courage was found in abundance within my being, but what was one to do if the sheer sight of the opponent magically made the knees turn to jelly? I was after all not trained for this sort of a duel.

I had to do something about the situation, and sometime soon, if I was to give myself any chance of reestablishing contact with my books and limiting the embarrassment that my grades were bound to bring.

"You would be staying here only during the preparatory leave?" it was Swati. She was going to stay at her uncle's place to prepare for the exams. Only three days of studying in peace, but a wise decision nevertheless – and suddenly an idea emerged out of nowhere.

"Yeah, I will be here only. Don't have any relatives here that I can go to and going home and coming back will eat up most of the time." *Now, now… ask her!!*

"Hey, I needed a small help. Is there a market or something close to where your uncle stays?" I was proud of the casual manner in which I had managed to hurl the words out.

"He stays in Delhi and not in some Amazonian Rain Forest. Of course, there is a market nearby. What do you want?" she shot back.

"Well, the summer vacations will be starting soon and I wanted to take back something for my cousin. And who better to pick it up, but you. Maybe an earring or a necklace or something? How much do you think that would cost?" I had about 2000 rupees in the bank account that my parents had opened for me with the branch on the campus (yes, we had our own Bank branch) and another couple of hundreds in cash. And left to me, I could have bought her the *Taj Mahal* with my little fortune.

"Well, a gold chain can cost anything from 7000 rupees upwards and silver earrings should be about 700 – 800 rupees. But then how old is she? If you want artificial jewellery, it can come for much lesser," she quizzed.

"She is almost our age and my budget is about a thousand rupees. So, I guess we can drop the necklace and stick to a nice pair of earrings. What do you think?" *Artificial jewellery; sounds so … artificial!! I am not going to start by gifting her anything artificial for sure.* With my limited knowledge of accessories meant for the fairer gender, I was glad to have found a subject matter expert to guide me through.

"Else you can settle for a pendant. You should be able to get a nice one within your budget?" I left the final choice between the pendant and earrings to her.

The fact that I had given two crisp 500 rupee notes to Swati for 'the gift already, made my decision much easier. I was going to propose to Ayesha. The burden had suddenly lifted from my chest and though

I was still thinking about her, my creativity was now mostly wandering around her expressions and the nice things she would have to say on receiving the gift. A possible rejection did not even occur to me and as if by some natural design, my thoughts refrained from venturing into uncomfortable territories. One positive outcome of this was that the respite from the internal tussle gave me a mental opening which I judiciously devoted to my books.

English was the first paper. Just after breakfast, Swati had handed me a small packet and some lose change. "It is a pendant. Let me know if you like it, else it can be changed also." I thanked her and quickly pocketed it, looking around to ensure that none of the boys had taken note of this little transaction.

It was a little later and within the confines of the closed toilet doors that I mustered the courage to look at the first gift for my love. It was beautiful. White metal twisted in the form of a three dimensional droplet with small stones making up the glitter of a dewdrop. She would look like a princess wearing it. I resigned it to my pocket with a satisfied smile. *Thank you Swati! Some day, when I tell my kids about how I proposed to their mom, you will have a prominent role to play in the story.*

Unlike regular classes, the seating arrangement during the exams was predefined and a rough seat map of the room with corresponding roll numbers had been drawn on the black board in wet chalk for reference. I had been allocated the third seat in second row. As I turned from the board towards my seat, the blood in my veins froze. There she was, hurriedly flipping through the text book for last minute revisions, looking like an angel, occupying the other seat on the desk that I had been assigned to.

"Hi," I wished her, placing my examination cardboard and stationary pouch on the desk.

"Oh… hi! So, you are roll no. 43? I hope you have prepared well. English is cool, but I am really scared of Maths and Physics," she said with a look that would have made me get her the moon, if she desired. Not knowing how to respond, I managed a, "Don't worry; I am sure you will manage. All the best!" *Only if you knew how well prepared I was. I could draw a mental picture of you blindfolded, but mathematical equations… sigh. But how does she intend to use my preparation in writing her exam?*

I got my answer soon. Twenty minutes into the exam and I noticed her skirt sliding upwards and exposing a part of her creamy thighs; only the creamy background was blemished with illegible scribbling. Her head down in a thinking posture, she was conveniently referring to her reference notes and possibly replicating a part of them on her answer sheet. *What a novel way to cheat! But, for a subject like English? Wonder what privileged extract of text she found worthy enough to be placed there… sigh!!* I watched in utter amazement as one thigh was concealed to reveal another scribbled one.

It was for the first time in my entire worldly existence that I was in such close proximity of any normally concealed portion of the female anatomy and it was casting a shenanigan on me. The near microscopic text created a tattoo like illusion and I had to murder my urges to reach out and feel the engraving. Nothing prevented me though from imagining her, thighs revealed, walking out to the shore from the sea – water glistering on her like fresh due; or dancing to the tunes of the latest blockbuster at a nightclub. Those thighs were evoking new depths of lunacy within me as I went about the motions of scribbling on my answer sheet with labored breath.

I have no clue as to how I fared in the exam and when the three hours of tussle between lure and restraint finally ended, I was exhausted to my bones. I now had to perform the most critical task of speaking with her and giving her the gift – I felt my pocket to ensure that its content was safe.

"See you tomorrow," she added as an afterthought while hurriedly picking up all the scattered stationary from the desk, submitting them to the confines of her bag and jetting out of the room. On examination days the buses continued to ply at their usual time, which meant that I had another two hours to locate her and do what I had to. *But she's already said a bye and gone. Wouldn't it look cheap if I were to track her down again and initiate a conversation? And, what would I speak to her about?*

The escapist within me was looking for reasons and there were enough and more for him to latch on to. *Yes, don't they say that it is better to be prepared? I need to rehearse my lines and figure out a way to find her alone, preferably after the exam tomorrow. I could do with some help. But who do I speak to?* I contemplated about having a word with Senti, but he in his state of near social abstinence was more than capable of sleeping though my narration, let alone being any help; and Swati, she would be difficult to explain my predicament to, more so since she thought that the pendant was a gift for my cousin. Bengali! I had my answer and I set out to look for the one elusive personality who could help me.

Bengali's penchant for preaching was now a known devil and I was hoping that by subjecting myself to it, I would at least manage some worthwhile ideas and the much needed motivation. After a good 20 minutes of looking around, I spotted him sitting on one of the benches next to the playground. He seemed to be deep in conversation with one of our day scholar classmates while happily gorging on the homemade *Parathas* from his Tiffin box.

"So, how was the paper?" I enquired, announcing my arrival.

"It was good. We were just discussing the same and it seems we have both done pretty well," he replied, extending the Tiffin box with a quarter of an *Aaloo Paratha* towards me.

"Here, have some. Delicious *Parathas.* Rohan's mother has made them." Bengali was known to have stolen Tiffin boxes and returned them empty to the bags of our unsuspecting classmates while the teacher had been busy teaching. By his standards, getting into a conversation with Rohan for the sake of emptying his lunchbox was hardly an effort and I was sure that with the contents of the box finished, their conversation and bonding would soon follow suit.

"Thanks Rohan. Let us get together to discuss the Chemistry paper tomorrow," he said, handing over the empty lunchbox to its rightful owner. "Let's see how the others have fared," that was my cue to help him make an escape and I gladly obliged, leaving a hungry but satisfied Rohan behind.

"Have you ever been in love?" I got straight to the point. "What kind of a question is that? Of course I have been. I love my parents, I love food and…"

"No. That's not what I meant. I meant the boy-girl kind of love. Have you ever fallen in love?" he took some steering to come on the right track, but when he did there was little stopping him. "What," he exclaimed, "Who is the lucky girl?"

"Wow, this is fabulous news. She is pretty neat… maybe a little snooty at times but I am sure you will manage to smoothen out the edges," he winked. "The problem is that how do I tell her all this? She hardly ever talks to me. And what do I say to her?"

"Don't be a fool my friend. These girls are like fish swimming in a pool of oil, you try to catch them and they are bound to slip out. You need to make them come to you instead."

"Bengali Baba, will you please cut the crap and tell me what I should be doing?" his incessant bantering was not going to help me.

I needed some concrete action steps to be outlined.

"Here is what we will do; you don't pay any attention to her tomorrow and I will catch her sometime and tell her that there is someone who is interested in her. Let the suspense build… get it? Suspense works like an aphrodisiac for these dames… It turns them on like no other thing. She will obviously get curious and plead for me to reveal your identity and I won't. We will let her live with the curios frenzy overnight and the next day, when she is on the brink of exploding under the suspense; I shall introduce you to her. What say?"

Barring the monumental exaggeration, his plan did have some substance. The best part of it was that he had taken the most important task on himself and I only had to make an appearance at the right time. "Bengal*i Baba* be praised. But do you think she will say a yes?"

"And, why not? Look at you, you are intelligent, no match for me but decent enough to look at and most importantly you are a hosteller. I mean, how can any girl in her right mind refuse to go around with a guy from the hostel?" He was right. Though, it wasn't as if the girls were queuing outside the hostel to get their hands on us, but we did evidently enjoy some sort of a privileged status when compared with the day scholars. I was in good stead and now in able hands too.

The next exam was chemistry and I had spent a better part of the previous evening conjuring images of my success outside the examination hall. It started as usual, her thighs doubling up as notebooks and she referring to the notes with a dexterity that I had first witnessed only on the preceding day. This time though, the thighs were aided by numerous paper chits that she seemed to extract from nowhere. I was busy noticing and admiring her antics when I saw her look at me with searching eyes. *Shit, shit!! She caught me looking at her. I bet she is thinking of me as some despicable pervert now.*

Instinctively I looked the other way and started to curse myself. "Psst..," I heard a faint whisper followed by a slight nudge on my ribs. The touch felt like it was always meant to be; only she could have done better than poking me with her elbow. I looked at her and she dragged my gaze to the question paper where her pen was steadily tapping on a particular question. It was some chemical equation that we were supposed to balance. *I need to help her. I need to help her.* No prizes for guessing though that the equation had remained unbalanced on my answer sheet as well. I gave her a nod, signaling for her to hold on and she happily returned to her faithful chits.

I needed that one answer like I had wanted no other. I looked around; all my classmates were busy pouring their brains out on paper. "Hey," I tapped the guy in front as soon as the invigilator turned her back towards me and he quietly leaned back to come within an earshot of my whisper. "4-a?" I had barely blurted out the question number when the invigilator turned around. "You! Stand up," she screamed.

"Me?" I quizzed, glancing to my left and to my right, making as innocent a face as I could.

"Yes you. Why were you talking?" she clearly was in no mood to fall for my I-know-nothing look. "But… I wasn't talking," I tried the next line of defense.

"You think I am lying? Look at your cheek! I saw you speaking to him," she said before shifting her attention to the boy in front, "What was he saying?" "I was only asking for a pencil," I immediately retorted.

The boy in front was someone who could be relied to provide you with the correctly balanced chemical equation but not a sound excuse in times of crisis – that required one to think on his feet. So, for my own sake I had to supply him with a story that could serve as our common line of defense.

"You think you are too smart? Give me your answer sheet… RIGHT NOW," she was almost trembling with rage. I didn't have an option. I couldn't apologize and beg; not with Ayesha looking at me with those grateful eyes. I was her hero. I had risked my own exam to provide her with one answer and now I couldn't bear to let her see me begging for mercy. Moreover, I was done writing about 30 minutes back and didn't think that I could add any more value to the paper in front of me in the little time that was left. So, I valiantly surrendered my answer sheet and walked out of the room.

Half an hour of mindless strolling in the campus and eventually the examinees started emerging from classrooms like a swarm of locust. "Hey, hope you managed to write enough before she took away your paper?" Senti asked, emerging from the crowd. Just then I spotted Bengali and Ayesha heading towards the canteen, deep in conversation.

"Uh.. uh.. Yes, I think I did," I replied, looking at Bengali searching for any kind of a hint about the progress he was making. He didn't even look at me. I continued to hold Senti in some senseless conversation till I saw them emerging again, ice cream cones in hand. He did not look at me again. *The Buggar! I am sure he has made the poor thing buy him ice cream.*

The perks that he managed to extract for himself aside, Bengali was a man of action. If there was one thing you could be assured about any task he undertook, it was that he would give it his best shot. "Dude, you owe me a big treat. I think you are on," he came back announcing his victory in ten odd minutes after I had last seen him, which incidentally would also have been the time he took to polish off his ice cream. "What happened? What did you tell her and what did she have to say?"

"I told her that there was someone interested in being friends with her and she obviously wanted me to disclose your identity, which I courteously refused. She started nagging me for clues then, 'Our class? From the hostel?' etc. And then, she came out with a guess and you won't believe whose name that was. It was you my friend, YOU!!" It could have meant just about anything, maybe I had given too much away through my heroics earlier in the day or maybe she had read through the innocent glances that I permitted myself to indulge in. "Will you please tell me all of it? How were her expressions when she took my name? What did she say after that?"

"Hold your horses my friend; the story only gets better from here on. Of course, without revealing your identity, I asked her for a reaction presuming it was you and she said… 'He seems like a nice guy. But why doesn't he speak to me himself.'… So there my boy, the stage is all set and I think it is time you made your entry." Now this was good news for sure. Breaking away from him, I headed towards the bus stop where the largest group of students could be seen loitering. I still had about half an hour to make some progress of my own, a third of which I wasted in locating her. She was sitting on a bench close to the bus stop and studying, presumably for the next exam.

"Hi, can I join you?" my sudden intrusion almost startled her. I soon realized that her reaction might have resulted from the fact that she was busy preparing her little chits for the next paper and obviously didn't want to be seen doing it by all and sundry. *Why not wait till you reach home and prepare them in some place a little private than the school bus stop?* "Ya… ya, sure. In fact I was looking for you. I am so sorry for what happened. I mean, I thought that you knew the answer and so I had asked you."

"Not a problem," I said, flashing my 440 watt smile and placing myself next to her on the bench. "Actually, I also wanted to have a word with you. You know, you are a pretty sweet girl and … I mean, we could… If we became friends, we could have a lot of fun." Now that I look back at what I managed to blurt out despite days and days of rehearsing, I can't help but feel embarrassed; there were a 1000 other things that I could have said, but… sigh. Anyways, as long as the ends justify the means, nothing else matters. "But we are friends, aren't we?" she responded with a puzzled expression that girls are known to have mastered over the years.

"Well yes, but I meant real good friends. I mean spending more time with each other and getting to know each other better," I explained, taking the little box out of my pocket. "And here is a little something I got for you. Hope you like it."

"You didn't have to," she said, opening the box. "Wow, it's beautiful. Thanks, but you shouldn't have," she shifted her gaze from the pendant towards me without making an effort to return it. Swati's selection had done the trick.

"Well, now that we are friends, why don't we grab a *Pepsi*?" I tried to make the most of the moment and also change the topic, making it easier for her to accept my first present. Since the drivers were already hovering around the buses, we decided to postpone the soft drink to the next day and after dropping her to the bus, I headed back to the hostel – gliding on a cloud of exhilaration and contentment.

The hostel grapevine was soon on an overdrive and I got a taste of its speed when Senti asked me about Ayesha as soon as I returned to my room after lunch. "So, did you finally propose to her," even sans the sarcasm in his tone, I knew that he was hurt and rightfully so. *Bloody Bengali, couldn't even mind his guts for a few minutes.*

"I was meaning to tell you, but didn't want to burden you any further," the excuse was sounding lame even to my own ears. I had been his only confidante and he deserved to know. "You should have told me, but never mind. Tell me, did you speak to her or not?" He seemed to have sensed my guilt and probably decided to ignore my gaffe. I was glad as I began recounting the developments from earlier in the day, infused with a liberal dose of my feelings, emotions and analysis.

The next few days of my life can be best compared with a rollercoaster ride. Struggling to spend time with books while hatching schemes to be able to spend more time with Ayesha; learning to handle the prying queries and frivolous comments from my hostel mates, all of whom seemed to be aware and interested in the recent change in my relationship status and generally learning to come to terms with my newfound love; it was all extremely taxing for a novice like me.

Neither of us had said the three magical words to each other, but at the same time we were both aware of the responsibilities and commitments that the 'being very good friends' tag came with. This was an accepted form of proposal within the campus and meant that those venturing into such a 'friendship' were fine with giving each other a fair chance at getting into a serious liaison – a trial phase of sorts. Girls not interested in having anything to do with a boy proposing for such a 'good friendship' were known to have countered it with 'I need time to think' or in extreme cases even an 'I am sorry, but I am not interested.' And since Ayesha had not retorted to any of those or any other accepted forms of denial, it was now up to me to prove myself and pass the test.

The test essentially comprised of two sections – one: ensuring that while in school, the girl spent most of her time with you, cementing your relationship in the eyes of the others and dissuading any other interested parties from making advances and two: ensuring enough top of the mind recall through late night phone calls, letters, greeting cards etc. I was faring respectably on the first count, the ongoing exams giving us enough time to be seen together in public and the hostel grapevine doing its own bit to spread the news. It was the second expectation that posed a major problem.

We were not allowed to keep mobile phones in the hostel and though there were aberrations to every rule, I was solely dependant on the lone pay-phone in the campus for my calls. I had spotted some seniors wielding mobile phones but generally their existence remained under wraps for the fear of confiscation. And if anyone in my immediate circle possessed one, they had successfully prevented its existence from becoming public knowledge.

The pay-phone gobbled up a Re 1 coin every 2 minutes and I had seen some of the known lover boys of the hostel exchange Rupee 100 notes for a bagful of change from the canteen. They would remain glued to the phone for hours, detached from the world around them, making cooing noises. On one occasion I had been within earshot of such a conversation for a good ten minutes and had only heard the word 'No' being repeated at least a dozen times with varying degrees of emphasis on its two constituent alphabets and fluctuating sweetness in the tone – an *Operaesque* experience. I had wondered over the triviality of such an indulgence until I found myself competing with the very same bunch of people for my turn to make contact with my lady love.

Over the next week, I managed two sleepless nights and six successful hours of telephonic conversations with my beloved. Suddenly I knew what made the telecom sector in India one of the fastest growing one and the mystery of what lovers spoke about for hours together lay unraveled. They spoke about nothing. We spoke about nothing. The important thing was to remain connected, albeit over a digital medium; to hear her breathe, to conjure mental images of the scenery on the other end of the line – she, lying flat on the bed, clinging on to the receiver, staring into oblivion with dreamy eyes. *Sigh*.

"Atul, hold on a sec, I want to have a word with you," Swati called out to me. The last examination had just concluded and I was heading towards the hostel to get rid of my school bag before meeting Ayesha in the canteen. I knew that these were possibly one of the worst exams I had ever written, but the fact that they were finally over enveloped me with a sense of rudimentary relief.

"Hey, what's up?" I replied cheerfully, generously ignoring the fact that the interruption was eating away into the little time I had with my lady love. She looked unusually somber.

"The pendant that I got for your sister, I noticed that one of our classmates has been wearing it for the past few days," she said, looking at me with hurt eyes. I had not anticipated this twist and struck by a momentary feeling of guilt, like an errant child who had been caught red handed stealing a cookie from the jar, I wanted to subside into any recess I could find.

"Oh, you saw it," there was no point inventing another set of lies to defend one, and I settled for an attempt to make light of the situation. "You know how it is. I didn't know how it would shape up, so I thought I would tell you once things were a little clearer," I said with a sheepish grin. She seemed to be buying none of it and continued to size me up with her probing eyes. "You know, it could have been a little embarrassing if Swati had declined," I justified.

"I didn't expect this from you. I always thought of you as a good friend and would have expected you to tell me the truth. Anyways, that's still ok, but telling me that the gift was for your sister, while you always wanted it for that… that… Ayesha? How do you explain that?" The scorn in her voice was evident, though I couldn't quite figure out whether it emerged from my misdeed or the fact that its beneficiary was Ayesha.

"Ok, I am sorry, *baba*. Won't happen again. Now forget it and tell me; through with your packing? When are you leaving?" The one thing that could get a hostellers mind off anything in the world was the thought of going home; minus of course unfortunate ones like me, for whom it spelt into painful separation. What Swati intended to do with her summer vacation was not of any immediate interest to me, but it was the only means to put an end to this unexpected confrontation.

"I am leaving today evening," my ploy seemed to have worked before she began again after a brief pause, "It is ok, I understand, but did feel bad. You know, you should have told me."

"I know… I am sorry."

"And Ayesha, I mean she is pretty, alright, but are you sure about it? I mean, I know her and I don't think she is quite your type." I was prepared to apologize, sympathize and give whatever else it took to make this conversation end amicably, but this amounted to transgression. "Not my type… meaning?" I quizzed.

"Well, you are nice guy, sincere and ambitious, while she is one of those fast, high-flying, big-city girls. Not the best of matches, if you know what I mean?"

"No, I don't quite know what you mean. Just because I come from a small town, you think I am not good enough for her? Well, for your kind information, she has already accepted my proposal." *Alright, I did lie to her, but that doesn't give her the right to humiliate me.*

"That is not what I meant. I am your friend, not hers, and I would not want to see you get hurt tomorrow," she argued. "Let it be. Thanks for your concern, but it would be better if you mind your own business and leave me to take my own decisions. And thanks for getting me the pendant," I said before exiting the scene. *Not my type, yeah, my type would be someone who can milk a cow or make dung cakes, the nosey bitch! Where does she think she comes from anyways, New York City?*

I quickly brushed off the untoward face off from the slate of my thoughts. There were more important issues looming large ahead of me. I was to leave for home the same evening and a month and half of separation from Ayesha was superseding any excitement that emerged from the thought of meeting my parents or gorging on the delicacies from my mother's kitchen. I knew that the times ahead were going to be trying and as I saw the school bus steering out of the gate drawing her further from me, it felt as if someone was slowly pulling away my soul from the body. *Oh, how much I love her! How will I survive this separation? God, why can't two lovers be together, forever?*

Five

The chilly river water remains a phobia till such time that you jump into it and similarly the pain of my separation lost its sting as I submerged myself into the languid days of my summer vacation. The initial days were tougher as I would suddenly find myself drifting into thoughts of my beloved at no particular time of the day, distracting me from the most mundane of chores. I was bumping into furniture; staring at ceilings and making people repeat what they said at an alarming frequency; leaving me with a very worried mother to contend with.

"Is everything alright? If you are facing any problems in the school, tell me and I will get your father to bring you back," her offer would have been lucrative had it not been for Ayesha and finding myself unable to resolve the predicament, I continued to dismiss her concerns as mere nothings.

Ayesha was spending the first two weeks of the vacation with her maternal uncle and his family in *Gujarat*, which meant that we couldn't even speak over the phone. Though she had offered to call me as and when she could, I had vetoed the suggestion for the fear of exposing my little secret to my parents; and how I was cursing myself for it. The frustration arising out of my helplessness in being able to reach out to her peaked and then settled as I started adjusting with the separation. Soon things started to normalize and her thoughts only surfaced in the confines of my room, to silently usher me into the realms of sleep.

Once she returned to Delhi, I made it a point to call her once every two or three days and disconnect the line if an unknown voice answered. The three times that I managed to speak to her comprised of two brief chit-chats, her family presumably depriving her of the much needed privacy and the only mention-worthy conversation when she went on and on about her trip.

"I am missing you. Why can't this darned vacation end earlier?" she had sweetly cooed, words that incessantly echoed within me for the remaining period of detachment, adding a spring to my stride and a few additional millimeters to my smile. *She was missing me too. She loves me just as I love her.*

As if the gods were paying serious attention to her words, the vacation ended in no time and I soon found myself back in the school campus, sweet memories of the past swarming me from all directions. Once in the confines of my room, I whipped out my mobile phone

– one of the two identical instruments I had recently bought, driven by the very real fear of not being able to communicate with her and the near blackmail that made my mother cough up the means to buy them, and dialed her number.

"I know we are not allowed to keep mobile phones, but everyone in the hostel has one. I will keep it safely in my cupboard and only use it at night to speak with you. You don't know how lonely it gets and there is no other way that I can speak to you when I want to." The emotional spiel had worked and after a bit of haggling, I had managed to extract 8000 rupees from her to buy myself a mobile phone.

And it was indeed the first task I did on disembarking from the bus in Delhi. I bought not one, but two handsets worth 4000 rupees each and used some of the money my father had given me for two prepaid connections. *It might not be the best handset in the market and she certainly deserves much better, but given the limited resources, this will at least permit us to talk at will. I hope she likes it.* The phone went unanswered and I had to resign myself to waiting for the next morning to hear her voice.

Ayesha was ecstatic. "It is fabulous. You didn't have to, but I am so excited. We can now talk for hours without worrying about my parents waking up," she had said on discovering the contents of the package that I had quietly slipped into her school bag. "Urrggghhh… you deserve a kiss for this, but…," she shrugged, panning around to signal at the crowd of people around us, enjoying the recess. *Shit, shit… If only I knew!! I would have saved it for another day when we were not being trampled over by a sea of humanity. There goes my first kiss.*

I was happily basking in the glow of my newfound love, spending every possible minute of the school time with Ayesha, sending her text messages once she left and late night telephonic conversations which could no longer be termed as 'general'. We discussed our longings, our wants and listening to her express her desire to hug me left me craving for even more.

The word had spread and every living soul in the campus who knew either of us, now knew that we were together. There was enough and more of leg-pulling and teasing that my hostel mates subjected me to, but with an undertone of acceptance that made me feel accomplished. We no longer had to keep our relationship hidden and though there was no formal graduation from being 'good friends' to being lovers, both of us, like the rest of the school, knew that we were in a relationship.

Senti had been intently following my love life and would wait for me to share with him the latest twists and turns. In fact I had a fleeting suspicion, for no apparent reason though, that his extra attentive ears made up for his shut eyes when I was busy with my late night conversations with Ayesha. I couldn't tell if it was the ointment of time or the time spent at home during the summer break, but Senti seemed to have negotiated his way out of the self imposed shell rather well. He was back to being his usual self and had also started using the balcony for his afternoon study sessions; a time I had conveniently devoted to my siesta.

In the midst of all the excitement came the dreaded examination result. As expected, I had barely crossed the passing barrier in most subjects but for two and while my English marks were pulling my average above the danger level, Mathematics was a red blot on my card. Despite all the clandestine assistance, Ayesha had also managed to flunk Maths and Physics – a result that would have shaken the sturdiest of individuals but had left her completely unperturbed. I knew that the two remaining terms were good enough for me to cover up, but I was worried about her making it to the next grade.

"You worry too much. I will manage. By the way, I am joining the extra classes for mathematics and physics. Are you joining any too?"

Extra classes were provided to students who had not performed well in particular subjects during the term exams, so as to bring them up the curve and in line with the rest of the class. The classes were held after the normal school hours and the day scholars were expected to make their own arrangements to travel home – a legitimate way for love birds to spend more time together and with a drastic reduction in the number of prying eyes around.

"Of course, I am joining mathematics and physics," I said, sneaking in a quick wink. "My, my… Hasn't someone become naughty?" she said, playfully tugging me in the ribs.

My afternoon siesta was the first victim that the extra classes claimed and the second, well almost, was my virginity. We had our extra classes three days of the week, one day for each subject and a day when we had a class each for both the subjects. We were in our third week of relishing the extra time that we got with each other, when instead of the canteen – our usual hangout; Ayesha led me towards the junior school building. We only had a physics class to attend that day and we had over an hour to ourselves, so I followed her without questioning our deviation from the normal route.

"Here, let me show you something," she said, signaling towards the adjoining squash court. The building that housed the court was an independent structure in between the junior school building and the swimming pools. Though the intent behind constructing it might have been noble, the game had not found much fervor among the students and for a better part of its existence, it stood like an isolate, uninhabited sore, plaguing the otherwise bustling landscape. In fact in my past few months on the campus, I had never felt the need to venture into the building and neither had I seen anyone making an entry or an exit. And in the middle of the afternoon, when even the otherwise bustling school buildings were deprived of much human activity, the last place one would want to go to was the squash court. Unless of course, the purpose was to make the most of the seclusion that it offered.

Stuffing the precipice of uncertainty with hopeful images of my own conjuring, I let myself be guided up the stairs, till there was no place to go. A thick padlock on the terrace door informed us that we had reached a dead end, at least as far as the exploration of the building was concerned.

"Well, we have the place all to ourselves," she said, looking at me invitingly. It was not often that I found myself in situations such as these, (in fact this was my solitary experience in my many years of existence) and hence I decided to pass away conventions and obey spontaneity; a decision that my brain had a very limited role to play in. I grabbed her by the head and in one swift motion, pulled her closer to me, placing my eager lips on to hers.

I was searching within for the nervousness that had accompanied every mental image that I had formed of this very moment, but it was nowhere to be found. I was completely at ease, following my primal instincts and exploring her entire being with the hunger of a wild beast attacking his prey. The prey, not wanting to succumb without putting up a fight, was matching my every move with parallel intensity, making the hunt all the more exhilarating. She moved and wriggled and guided me with a vocation that was so fluid and on intuition that was so wise that a more suspicious man would have confused them with obvious experience.

Entangled like a pair of wrestlers, we dropped to the ledge leading up to the terrace door and continued with our struggle for one-upmanship in the duel. One after the other I was introduced to her silk textured skin, lines of fuzz, hidden moles and a body that would have delighted the most accomplished of sculptors, all of whom I had shamelessly imagined in the past. Once the initial euphoria settled, we were faced with the helpless humor that formed the spirit of our situation. As any individual who had opted for a bed of solid concrete set in 4x3 feet of confined space as the venue for his first real encounter with his beloved could vouch for, there was little scope for taking our bout to its logical conclusion; my inexperience acting as another significant deterrent.

I could feel my knees and elbows bearing the wrath of the concrete underneath, but not wanting to bequeath I continued with my struggle to mount my newfound throne till I heard an impish giggle from underneath.

"My tiger, haven't you had enough already? Let us save something for another day," she said, stroking my hair. Her tapered eyes of a carnivorous animal now had a tame and satisfied look to them. I was like a child who had been invited by Alice into her wonderland, only to be shunted out before he could experience the elixir of contentment. But I knew that the enchanted tour was over for now and I had to be satisfied with what I had got. We dressed up lazily and sneaked out of the building, making it just in time to hear the bell that announced the conclusion of the physics extra class.

I dropped her to the school gate and as she walked towards her waiting car, I pinched myself to ensure that all that had transpired was real and not a sequence out of a dream. The pain was for real. In a state of trance I returned to my room and pushed the door open to be greeted by a startled Senti, who, surprised by my sudden arrival, was trying to hide something under his thighs.

"The class got off early today?" he enquired with a familiar guilty tinge to his tone. He was sitting on his bed, possibly writing something in the notebook that now lay shut in front of him. *But what is it that he is hiding from me?* I looked towards his legs, which were doubling up as a shield to conceal his secret from me – Nothing; but I did catch a glimpse of a droplet of blood oozing from his wrist.

Suicide? Is the crazy ass trying to die up on me? "What the hell is this? What are you hiding?" I said, pulling up his wrist to expose the wound.

"Nothing," he said, trying in vain to pull his hand loose from my grip. He didn't succeed, but the tussle revealed the object of hiding – a geometry compass; a pointed instrument used to draw spherical shapes. I examined the cut on his wrist; it was just an abrasion, caused in all likelihood by the compass he was trying to hide. He was going to live alright, but not without a liberal dose of verbal reprimand that he had called upon himself. "Have you gone crazy? What is all this? You are trying to kill yourself or something?" I yelled.

"No, no… It is not what you are thinking. I was… I was… only writing a letter," he said in a manner that left no scope for suspicion. He was telling the truth. *A letter! But, what does slashing of a wrist have to do with writing a letter?*

He opened the notebook in front of him and pushed it towards me.I soon got my answers. On the open page, I saw large red alphabets scrawled to form a set of words. The idiot had been using his blood as ink, his hand as an inkpot and the compass as a pen to create this masterpiece. I picked up the notebook for a closer scrutiny of his handiwork. It read, "Dear Zehnab, You are the most beautiful thing to have happened to me. I love you. I am dying to meet..." He would have been working on the last sentence when my sudden appearance distracted him.

I sat down, clamping my head between my palms. "I think I have been missing something here. Now, will you please begin to educate me?"

Senti was a vulnerable soul, comfortable with his books but not so with the ways of the world. I was irritated at myself for not having kept a tab on him, a responsibility that had grown up on me over the past few months. I could bully him, scold him, scream at him and yet, I could not see him in harms way – a brotherly kinship that hostel roommates so often develop.

"I knew you would not be ok with it, so I didn't tell you. But she is a nice girl," he began; the narration well interspersed with justifications. I listened. "A few days after her first letter, she wrote to me again. She wanted to meet up. I was confused, didn't know what to do. Her thoughts had anyways been hounding me and the fact that she was also thinking about me made my decision simpler and we met."

"Where on earth did you guys meet? And when?" I knew that when smitten by the love bug, people have a tendency to see logic in the most abject acts of lunacy, but this was something else. There was no fathomable reason for a hosteller to engage into conversation with a family member of one of the laboratory assistants. Just being spotted together would have carried catastrophic implications for both of them, especially Senti. All god fearing brothers are programmed to detest any love interest that their sisters develop, and if Sharif somehow discovered, the least he would do is present the case to the hostel warden, resulting in Senti's suspension from the hostel – a best case scenario. *What has he been thinking?*

"She has started working at a retail store as a shop assistant. So we met at a coffee shop near her store on Saturday," Senti clarified. "She is a nice girl and both of us like spending time with each other." *At least he had the brains not to meet her within the campus, but...* "Spending time? But when on earth have you been spending time with her?"

The revelations were as shocking for me as the discovery of life forms on Mars. "We have been meeting on Saturdays mostly. Sometimes she manages to come to the terrace after dinner and we exchange letters. But that is not certain since she usually returns pretty late from work." Senti was clearly beyond the realms of logic and there was no point in trying to explain the futility of his engagements given the current state of his mind. As long as it did not pose an immediate risk, I could leave him to negotiate his own path and focus instead on the enchanting journey that my love life had embarked upon. *Ayesha... Oh, what would I do without you?*

"One of the girls was saying that she saw you and Ayesha coming out of the squash court the other day. You are hardly even in class nowadays. What's up with you?" Swati quizzed. The 'pendant' incident had been buried under the debris of time and we were back on cordial terms – she continuing to be her usual nosey self.

"All is well, nothing to worry about. Just that there are not many places in the campus that permit you to make personal conversation without being consumed by prying eyes and ears, so we would have been sitting near the squash court somewhere," I explained. "Making conversation? Is that what they call it now-a-days?" the scorn in her voice was apparent. *The meddling bitch!*

"And just what do you mean by that?" I was starting to lose my cool. "People are no fools. Everyone is talking about the two of you," she retorted.

"Well, people can talk as much as they wish to and anything that they want to, but as long as they are not talking about you, why are you even bothered? Or is it that you are jealous of me or something?" I owed her no explanations and she had no right to come prying into my personal space.

"I told you because I thought you should know. That is what friends are supposed to do. But I guess, you are too preoccupied in life to understand any of it," she said before storming off. *I need to maintain safe distance from this one. She seems to be getting these attacks of dementia a little too frequently. Someone needs to teach her a thing or two about 'minding her own business.'*

Life was one big revelry; a bundle of fun and frolic and I was relishing it to the hilt. Passing love notes to her during class, sneaking up to the squash court and making merry, tens of text messages - significance of the information being exchanged conveniently overshadowed by the emotions behind the act, our midnight tête-à-tête, all of it was an experience that went beyond the limitations of words. She had sneaked into my life and had taken control over it like a happiness inducing drug and I was basking in ecstasy.

It was Saturday and Senti had left for his 'tuitions', ending the fifteen minutes of torture he had started subjecting the poor helpless mirror to, this day of every week. The warden had bought his story of having to attend some off-campus tuition classes every Saturday – a stroke of genius, ensuring that he didn't have to come up with a silly excuse every time he wanted to leave the campus and be with his beloved. The bearings of the scheme had been put together so discreetly that I had missed noticing them until I had accidentally stumbled upon his little secret. And now, I could not help but admire the precision in planning and the flawless execution of the plot.

He returned at his usual time just after lunch and without a word, collapsed on his bed – an unusual occurrence. He had been returning from his dates, a bundle of energy, eager to share with me the minutest of details of every mention worthy happening. How she held his hand or how she gave him a peck on his cheek, he would be bubbling with excitement and wouldn't stop raving about her. Today however, he seemed sapped and completely drained out. "What happened? She didn't turn up or what?" I enquired.

"No, no. She came, but I don't know. I am just a little confused," he murmured. "Why? What happened?"

"Her family wants to marry her off. There is this guy, apparently a distant relative of theirs and all going well, she thinks in a few months she will get married," he said, desperately controlling his tears.

"Hey, relax. You always knew that this didn't have a future; with your age, religion and all that. There is little that you can do at this stage. Just relish the good times that you have spent and you can always remain friends with her. I know it is easier said than done but there really is no point in crying over something that you can't really control."

"She doesn't want to marry him. She wants to be with me," he objected.

"I understand, but you need to explain to her that no matter how you guys feel about each other, this thing had to end sometime," I continued to console him. "That is not the point. I told her all of that and it only flared her up. She wants me to speak to my parents about her," he said.

"What? Have you lost it? You are all of 17. How can you even think of something like that?" I almost yelled, hoping that the high pitch would find some resonance with his love infested system.

"I am scared," he said, for the first time looking me in the eye, "I can't marry her. I can't even tell my parents about her, but she doesn't understand. She said that if I was not willing to commit, I had no right to play with her feelings and that she will not let me go so easily."

"What do you mean?" this was more serious than it seemed at the onset. "Atul, (he had called me with my real name in place of 'Jaat Bhai' – an indication that he was genuinely disturbed) she says that I have used her and if I don't tell my parents about her soon, she will be forced to tell her family about me. I don't know what to do, she has all my letters, which she says she will show to the hostel warden and also to my parents. I am finished," he said before the dam containing his tears collapsed and he broke into a hysterical sob.

"I liked her, but I never thought it would come to this. I should have listened to you, but now it is too late. I didn't know she could stoop down to.. to.. blackmailing me."

If ever there was a grave situation, this was one. She had led him on and an unsuspecting Senti had eagerly gobbled up the bait, landing himself in a soup. "But you have her letters too," I tried to reason, knowing fully well that the case was not open to judicial scrutiny and having no amount of favorable evidence was going to help. His parents, who were living under the delusion that their son was preparing hard for his entrance examinations were not likely to take this well, and if the warden did not expel him from the hostel, there was every chance that they would voluntarily drag him back home. And if at all he managed a miraculous escape somehow, his reputation in the school and the hostel was sure to take a fatal blow.

"She.. She even blamed me of wanting to get physical with her. I swear Atul, I had no such intentions. The only time that we kissed was at her behest," he seemed devastated. "I know, I know. Just try and relax a bit and we will find a way out of this," I said, comforting him with an embrace. It took a while but finally he sobered down and we got around to figuring out the next steps. Various options, ranging from confronting Sharif to involving Senti's parents were discussed before being dropped. It was almost dinner time and we had no clue as to how we should go about handling the situation.

"You think we should have a word with Bengali?" I suggested. Bengali was like a cat left in charge of a milk bowl when it came to secrets, but he had something that we needed the most – a brain capable of finding an answer to the most hopeless of problems. An appeal to his humane side, if at all there was one, and who knows he might actually be capable of keeping a secret too. We had both exhausted our grey cells with nothing concrete to show for it and the risk seemed minuscule in light of the situation we were confronted with. Senti consented, albeit amid some degree of weary reluctance and we very nearly dragged our savior to our room after dinner.

It took me a good half an hour to narrate the entire episode and Senti filled in when I missed out on some critical facts. "Did you guys make out?" a very thoughtful Bengali finally spoke. "It is an important piece of information to determine the gravity of the situation. Don't fuckin bore a hole into me with your looks," he responded to the menacing gaze his question elicited from me.

"No. As in, we kissed once and held hands and all that, but nothing much," Senti answered. "There is more to it than meets the eye," Bengali said, sounding important and creating suspense in his trademark style. "Stop imitating a c-grade detective and get to the point. What do you mean by, 'there is more to it'?" I shot back.

"Tell me something; when you got her letter, you guys immediately knew that this thing was not going to work out. Then how come she continued to pursue Senti when she also knew that he was still in school and definitely much younger than her?" he addressed me. "I am sure she also knows that Senti is not going to marry her, no matter what. Why is she retorting to such tactics then? I mean, what will she get by ruining his life? I don't know, the picture doesn't look complete," he added before turning to Senti. "Had she ever mentioned marriage before this?" this time his question was directed towards him.

"No, this was the first time that we spoke about anything concerning marriage," he replied. Bengali had a point. It could be argued that she was also fascinated by Senti and wanted to spend time with him, but blackmailing him to tell his parents about their relationship, when she knew that his parents would never agree to them being together, was beyond any fathomable logic. "Give me some time to think this through and let us talk about it tomorrow. In the meantime, just think if there is anything she ever mentioned that might give her a reason to harass you or anything that she might want from you."

He finally left, leaving behind a situation that seemed even more complicated now than when he had walked into the room. "I can't understand why…?" Senti said before switching off the lights. "Good night to you too," I replied. *Poor Senti!! Girls can be so bloody unpredictable. Zehnab, and not to forget that bitch Swati… phew. Thank God that Ayesha is nothing like them.*

six

The winter season in Northern India was no stranger to me, but this time round it seemed to have surfaced with a renewed vigor. The mercury was dipping like a spent fire cracker and the sun appeared to be pleasuring from the game of hide-and-seek; its new-found pastime for most mornings. Amidst the dysfunctional geysers and smelly decaying quilts, the hostel had its own ways of dealing with the chill.

The consumption of deodorants had shot up while the early morning bathing queues had diminished remarkably diminished. Amid many more illegal possessions, coiled electric heaters had surfaced in most rooms, leading a life of dual utility – spreading warmth and acting as a stove for late night meals and brews meant to resemble tea, coffee or soup. The meals comprised of bread and butter smuggled from the hostel mess and even the make shift utensils bore the school insignia; nimble and clandestine exports from the mess that often went unnoticed.

Ayesha was still lurking about in my thoughts before I went off to sleep, but cuddling up inside my quilt and thinking about her was a more pleasurable experience than doing so under the continuous hypnotic movement of the ceiling fan. Sitting with her during the school break, soaking in the sun and feasting my eyes on her while she lazily licked her ice cream cone; watching her rub her hands against each other and blow on them with an inviting pout – the season came with its fair share of enchantments.

"… the weekend after next. You think you will be able to manage permission to come out?" she and a few of her friends from the colony were planning a weekend trip to *Agra*. Since the two other girls were coming with their boyfriends, Ayesha wanted me to accompany her as well.

"I stay in a hostel and not *Tihar Jail*, I will do something. Don't worry," I said, playfully stroking her hair. My parents would surely have flipped if they came to know that I was planning a weekend outing with a girl, in fact they were likely to flip if they came to know even half the things that I had been engaging in off late. *These girls, their parents must be what they call 'open minded' – allowing their daughters to go for weekend outings with their boyfriends. Or, maybe they are just not as well informed about the group's composition as I am. Who the fuck cares, this is going to be fun!*

Though a full week separated me from the escapade, I was already giddy with excitement and dreaming about all that could and if lady luck willed, would happen. Mechanically, I finished my lunch and was walking out, trying to focus on the pervasive need of coming up with a believable story for the warden when I was intercepted by Bengali. "You know what. I think this girl has some ulterior motives. Maybe she is trying to extract money or something," he conspiratorially whispered. *Ayesha? Who is she trying to extract money from?*

It took me a few seconds to emerge from my wonderland and recollect the immediate hurdle that we had in front of us. He was not talking about Ayesha. It was Zehnab that he was referring to. "What makes you say that?" I reasoned with him, buying time to come up with a quick analysis of my own. I was guilty of having let Senti fall into this trap and now I had even managed to conceal his problems within some unfrequented recess of my mind. A tinge of guilt surfaced and soon got trampled under Bengali's analytical reasoning.

"For a second let us assume that she actually loves him – then instead of trying to appeal to his love for her, why would she retort to blackmailing him? I am sure she knows that by doing this she is negating any chances that might have been there of him willingly talking the same language as her. And if they are not going to be together then why make him go through all this unnecessary mental masturbation?" He had a valid point. "She obviously doesn't come from a well to do family and would know that someone who can afford the hostel fees would be coming from a reasonably wealthy background. If she wasn't after money, why would she first woo Senti and then threaten him with the things that are likely to scare him the most – involving his parents and the warden?"

"But how can we be sure?" his hypothesis made sense, but I didn't want to commit to it till the time we figured out a way to test it. "I have an idea…," he replied with a mischievous grin.

The biggest hurdle in the way of our plan was going to be its beneficiary, Senti. Though shaken and taken aback by the turn of events, he was still concealing a sizeable chunk of love for Zehnab in some remote corner of his heart and it was not going to be easy getting his buy-in for testing Bengali's hypothesis.

As expected, his first reaction was marginally short of qualifying as violence. "You guys are fucking crazy. She said a lot of things that she shouldn't have said, but this… this is taking things to a different level. How did you guys even conceive something so… so atrocious? She loves me and wants to be with me and obviously might have overreacted in the heat of the moment. Just because of that, you can't go about doubting somebody's integrity," he had nearly freaked out on our suggestion.

"We are not doubting her integrity or saying that she is a bad person, but the developments certainly don't add up. If there is something that we can do to get a clearer picture of things, what is the harm in doing it? What have we got to lose and what other options do we have anyways? You can keep sulking and screaming at us and she will happily have you packed off to Jharkhand and marry the other chap" Bengali said, defending our stand. "What if she doesn't turn out the way you guys are assuming she would? What would I do then?" this was a question that we hadn't quite managed an answer to as yet.

The entire plan was based on the premise that Zehnab was the quintessential daily-soap vamp who was behind Senti only for his money. If she turned out to be just another over reacting, heart broken girl, we ran the risk of complicating the situation even further. "And what if she is too smart to fall for it?" I had voiced my concern when Bengali had first shared his idea with me.

"It can't leave him in any worse stead than he is in today. And if it actually doesn't go as planned, we can always think of something else, but for now can you think of a better alternative?" his arguments had been enough to convince me but sounded frail in front of Senti, who was also supposed to deliver the bait – a critical ingredient of the plan.

One thing that worked in our favor though was that Senti could not imagine confiding in his parents about his current situation which left him with a near desperate shortage of options. So, after an hour of logical reasoning, debate and emotional spiel, Senti reluctantly conceded to playing his part as directed. He had a few nervous pangs and change of minds in the interim, but importantly, come Saturday he was ready to deliver. We wished him luck, and like a valiant warrior he left to conquer his destiny while we retired to my room, waiting to perform our part.

As he later claimed, Senti played his part well, telling her a fabricated story of having spoken with his parents about her. "I spoke with my dad. We had a big argument over the phone. He was not willing to listen to anything that I had to say and was adamant that I cut off all ties with you. He is not a bad person, you know. Just that he loves me a lot and wants me to have the best possible life, but in a manner he conceives to be right," he had started with his well rehearsed speech as soon as they took their seats in the coffee shop. She listened intently, not spilling her reactions in the interim.

"However, when he suggested that I offer you money for going your own way and leaving me alone, I completely lost it. How could he even say something like that?" this was when he was supposed to pause and make a dramatized effort to contain his tears. If anything, he was a pathetic actor and it was only about the tenth time or so that he had managed this piece with traces of conviction during our practice sessions. During the actual performance though, he claimed to have got it right in the first and only take and thankfully so.

"Adults have their own way of thinking which is not always in line with our thoughts, but I am sure he would have said it with your best interest in mind. We can't expect him to understand what we share, can we?" she had replied calmly.

"At this point I thought we were done. Her concern was so touching that I knew we had misjudged her. I didn't know how I was going to get myself a dad who would go and meet up with her family. I knew that I had been an ass to even listen to your stupid idea and I could see myself drowning in the soup you had thoughtlessly stirred," Senti was liberal with his accusations while narrating the incident to us, "but I decided to carry on with the plan nevertheless, more so because I couldn't think of anything better to say or do."

"I do understand his point now, but then I was furious and ended up yelling at him. It was the first time ever in my life that I would have spoken to him in such loud voice. I disconnected the phone and we didn't speak for a couple of days, but then I needed him to understand my perspective and so I called him again. This time though he was reasonably receptive and said that he would meet up with your family, if that was what I wanted. Parents are such an amazing gift that at times I wonder if they come from the same world as us. When it comes to their children, they are always willing to scale any possible length and more… sigh. So, check with your family and let me know. I will call my folks over to Delhi when it suits them."

The first scene had been executed well; Senti had briefly mentioned his father's suggestion about paying her off and based on her reactions, he was to reinforce the bait by dropping an astronomical figure during the course of normal conversation. Driven by the fear of involving her own family and the lure of the bait, she was expected to express her favor for his father's point of view and this was when we were to come into action. Senti would call on my mobile from a nearby payphone and Bengali would talk to her posing as his father.

He would make her feel comfortable by explaining how for her the right thing to do would be to leave Senti alone and accept the money. He would raise the stakes if necessary and since the amount was purely imaginary, there were no budgetary constraints that had to be kept in mind. Eventually when she accepted the offer, Bengali would tell her that their conversation had been recorded and if she did not dismiss all contacts with Senti with immediate effect, he would have her arrested on charges of blackmail. The conversation was not being recorded (there were some mobile handsets that came with such a functionality, but mine was a basic version) and neither did we have the money to pay her, the plan solely depended on the magnified sense of fear that every crooked plan instilled in the minds of its perpetrator.

The ball was in her court now. Her demeanor did not betray any emotions and after a thoughtful pause, she finally spoke. "I know you love me a lot and I am sorry for saying a lot of things the other day. I know I have hurt you, but you know that I didn't mean any of those things, right?" she looked at Senti in a manner that 'made his heart melt.' "I wanted to give her a tight hug just then, but we were in a coffee shop so I nodded," he reminisced.

"I have been terribly confused and despite a lot of thinking since our last conversation, was not being able to see things straight. However, now I am convinced. Santosh, you mean a lot to me and it is difficult for me to imagine a life without you and I know that you love me too. But there are others who also have a stake in our lives and I don't think we have the right to trample over their expectations and love – that would be an extremely selfish thing to do. Do you think you will be able to stay happy with me despite knowing that you have achieved this at the cost of your parents pride and their love for you?" the question did not solicit an answer and Senti continued with the part of a silent listener.

"I am sure my family will have problems too. We are from different religious backgrounds, plus you are much younger than I am. I want to start a family with the blessings of my parents and not by giving them pain. Santosh, I think it is about time we parted ways," she concluded. The sense of momentary relief was washed away by a wave of emotions and Senti was actually in tears and he did not need any dramatics to come to his aid. "But…," was all he could contribute to the conversation.

"I know it is going to be difficult, but you have your entire life ahead of you. You are a great guy and I am sure you will get someone far better than me in your life. I am glad that we met and I will treasure our friendship till the last day of my life," she said, caressing his hands between her palms.

"I have quit my job and will be returning to my hometown in a few days. I don't know if I will say a yes for marriage as of now; it is a little too soon, but I am surely going to miss you. I will write to you whenever I can. Promise me that you will remember me and reply to all my letters," these were the last words that

Senti heard from her. The plan had achieved its desired outcome without even progressing into its final act.

Zehnab was not seen on the terrace of the staff quarters or anywhere else in the campus after that day. Senti would carry his books to the balcony every afternoon and sit there for hours longing to catch a glimpse of her and ultimately return laden with disappointment. She had gone away from his life, in all probability she had gone away from the city too, but she had left behind a set of questions that even the gifted Bengali *Baba* could not answer with certainty.

Was her change of heart an outcome of the fear of telling her family about Senti or was her initial outburst a result of the frustrated desire to be with the man she loved? Was she too rational in her thinking and had backed out when matters started getting out of hand or was it her irrationality that accounted for the ferocious pursuit of her longings in the first place? Was she the one who had set the trap for Senti or was she also an innocent victim to have fallen into the time-laid trap?

Senti had not spoken about Zehnab with either of us since that day, but we knew that he was anxiously waiting for the letter she had promised she would write. Bengali and I also refrained from talking about her, but there was an unspoken thread of guilt that bound us together – guilt emerging from the possibility of having terribly misjudged the callings of true love. *Life does not always pan out like a scripted feature of the celluloid. It contains in its realms, feelings and emotions that no amount of logic can ever explain.* We would never be privy to Zehnab's real thoughts and feelings, but not all questions in life go answered.

Senti was once again back in his cocoon. For those who hadn't quite figured him out yet, he was an introvert, a loner who liked to keep to himself, but some of us knew better – he was a normal human being, bruised by the repeated turbulences of his love life. As I had learnt from experience, these were times when he was best left to his own; plus I had other important concerns to address.

Getting the warden's permission to go out for the weekend wasn't as tricky as I had anticipated it to be. A sincere face, a story about having to visit an ailing aunt and he was happily scribbling his signature on the permission slip. *Wow, this was awesome. Two whole days, and well… nights too, with Ayesha!!*

I washed my favorite denims and t-shirts and gave them for ironing, I borrowed Bengali's leather jacket, I borrowed Senti's knapsack, I borrowed (actually 'took' would be more apt) a can of deodorant from one of the juniors, I withdrew money from my bank and whatever time I was left with at my disposal, I spent in thinking about Ayesha and the trip. This would have been one of the fastest weeks to pass in the history of mankind, for in what seemed like a blink of the eye, we were down to Friday.

My bag was already packed and immediately after lunch, I rushed out of the campus and hailed an *auto* for the *Greater Kailash*

Market – our rendezvous point. We were to assemble at McDonalds at 2.30 in the afternoon from where we were to drive down to Agra. A burger, a coke and a few more minutes later I checked my watch again, it was almost 3.00. Ayesha had taken the school bus back home and was to join me here after a quick change of clothes. Since she was the only person in the group I knew, I had no way of telling if our other companions were already inside the restaurant.

I scanned the surroundings looking for a bunch of people with bags or any other clue that could point me towards her friends. *What's the point? Even if I spot them, I am not going to walk up to them till she shows up. She could have sent me a message if she was getting late.* I had refrained from calling her since I knew that she would be busy dressing up and packing and I didn't want to be a pest. Also, the fact that I had only 20 odd rupees of talk-time left on my prepaid card helped with my restraint and just when I was on the verge of dialing her number, I heard my name being called out.

"Over here," she yelled from the entrance. She was here. It was 3.15 p.m. I got up, picking my bag from the next chair while she negotiated her way towards me. "Where were you?" I registered my annoyance. "Oh, Pragati and Sonali came over to my place, so Varun picked us up and then we picked up Abhay on the way. Come, they are all waiting for you in the car," she said, locking her hands with mine and just short of dragging me out with her.

The car was a *Honda CRV* and the owner, Varun was at the wheels. After a brief round of introductions we joined Abhay and Sonali in the rear section of the car while Pragati took up the seat next to Varun. In no time we were zipping past the unusually vacant roads, heading out of the city. "Beer?" Abhay handed me a can from the portable ice-box before collecting the empties from others and handing them refills. A *Punjabi* band was challenging the decibel levels in the vehicle while the occupants were straining their vocal chords to make conversation. Ayesha was squeezed between Sonali and me, and with every jerk I could feel her pushing further into me – I was not complaining.

Pragati and Sonali were the same age as us while Abhay was a year older. Varun was the eldest of the lot and was in his second year of a graduate course from the Delhi University. All of them seemed to know each other well and had ample topics to discuss – from common friends to the latest night spots in the city. The girls attempted to engage me in conversation with a, "we have heard so much about you from her," or, "have you been to the *Hard Rock Café*?" but I was happy listening to the merrymaking for a better part of the four hour journey.

We reached our hotel at about 7.30 and leaving the bags at the reception, headed for the restaurant straight away. The journey had taken a toll on everyone and we had unanimously voted for an early dinner before retiring to our rooms. The *Taj* would need to wait for another day.

Varun had taken care of the arrangements and we were all to contribute our share of the damages later. There were three rooms booked, one for each couple and like me, all the others seemed eager to recoil into the privacy with their respective partners. The half a dozen beer cans he had emptied and the whiskey he was sipping now was already having a visible impact on Abhay and he was finding it difficult to keep his hands to himself, caressing and touching Sonali at every possible pretext. I was feeling a little tipsy too. But my condition was like the newlywed groom, who tries hard to conceal the excitement of his first night in the garb of innocence and at times, lack of awareness about what lay in store – a stupid attempt at guising the inevitable and ducking embarrassing looks from the knowing eyes around.

The time finally came when I opened the door to our room, Ayesha in tow. Even before I could locate the electricity switch, she grabbed me from the rear and pulled me to the bed. I managed a smooth landing, padded by the comfortable mattress and her familiar body. *Damn the switch.* Was it the alcohol or just the situation, I couldn't tell, but we were soon exploring frontiers that our cramped love-nest in the squash court building had deprived us of. "Here, you might need this," she said handing me a pack of lubricated condoms. *Ayesha, always a bundle of surprises… sigh.*

I was consumed by a numbing sense of satisfaction at eventually having broken the atrocious siege of waiting and before my senses gave in to the need for sleep, the last memory I carried was of the ethereal truth of the wildest and most tenacious love we made. The next morning I got up with a touch of fatigue, a smile on my face and a naked Ayesha clinging on to me – I was no longer a virgin; we had finally become one. Instinctively, I reached out for her and planted a kiss on her forehead. She hummed something before frowning in her sleep and turning to the other side, leaving my smile stretched by another inch.

The next morning we met in the hotel restaurant for a lazy brunch before heading to see the *Taj Mahal* – the epitome of love induced splurgence; and what a sight it was. The grandiose monument, standing tall in its blinding splendor, welcoming six souls brimming with love – I was ecstatic. *I know now the intensity of love that would have inspired the idea of this monument. Only if…I too had the means.* "Ayesha-Mahal, that is what I shall christen the one I make," I whispered in her ears. "My, my… Isn't someone getting romantic?" she replied, playfully pushing me away.

The rest of the day went about in sight seeing, gorging on the local delicacies and shopping. I couldn't get enough of the city or of Ayesha and by the time we returned to the hotel, I could sense my stomach twitching at the thought that our little vacation would soon come to an end. I was itching to hold her and when Abhay suggested that we go to his room for a round of drinks, I had to control a strong urge to smack him where it hurts the most. Since there were no objections voiced, I soon found myself sipping a glass of Rum and Coke in his room, much against my wishes.

"Dumb charades anyone?" Ayesha suggested as she got up to refill her glass. "Dumb charades!! Grow up sweetheart, that's a game for kids. But we can play truth-and-dare if you wish to," Varun interjected, flooring a suggestion of his own. *And truth-and-dare is being included in the next Olympic Games!! How silly is that? A bunch of grown ups playing silly games when there is so much more one can do with this time.* However, majority prevailed yet again and I found myself answering inane questions about my earlier crushes and listening to equally ridiculous revelations from others.

"How many guys have you kissed so far?" the question suddenly grabbed my attention. It had been directed towards Ayesha by one of the girls. "Well, I can't remember the exact count, but maybe 4 or 5," she responded nonchalantly. The answer hit me like a blow. I knew that Ayesha would have had a past life and there was a likelihood that she had dated a guy or two as well, but the casual manner in which she was discussing it came to me as a shock. I was also jealous. I knew that those she was referring to were her past but I also knew that I was one of the five and that the others had touched her much before I had.

I was finding it difficult to focus on the game and desperately wanted to excuse myself. But at the same time I didn't want my action to be seen as a reaction to her revelation, especially in front of her friends. So I stretched and stretched, till Varun finally announced that he was tired and wanted to hit the bed. The party came to an abrupt halt and we receded to our respective rooms.

"What happened to you? You were hardly your usual self out there," she remarked. "Well, it is not the greatest of feelings to know that your girlfriend has been kissing so many people that she finds it difficult to maintain count," I had been containing my reactions for some time now and as soon as they spotted a fissure, they started oozing out uncontrollably.

"And just what do you mean by that? I have never questioned you on your past life and I don't think you should be questioning mine," she retorted. I knew that she was right but a part of me had been so deeply wounded that my reactions were dispossessed of any logic. "I don't go about kissing every other girl that I meet. You are the first girl that I have kissed and you know that very well. I have every right to be concerned about your past life if you have been on an uncontrolled kissing frenzy before meeting me," I continued spilling venom.

"Atul, it was just a game and I didn't want to look like an ass in front of my friends, so I might have exaggerated a bit. But the last thing I expected was this kind of a reaction from you. Do you think I am some kind of a slut?" she had started to bare the most deadly weapon in any woman's armory – her tears; and before I knew, I was virtually swimming in them. The pain, the jealousy, the anger were all forgotten and the only thing I could think of was some way to close the floodgates in her eyes.

I hugged her, she pushed me back; I apologized, she ignored; I tried to kiss her, she pushed me back again, continuing to deprive me of any opportunity to make up for my sin for over an hour. I was amazed at the amount of liquid that had emerged from her little frame and was wondering if I was staring at an answer to the water problem of Delhi, when her crying came to an abrupt halt with a series of loud sniffs – reminiscent of a motorbike with a faulty sparkplug. "I hate you," she said before reaching out and embracing me tightly. The contradiction between her action and words was confusing, but it was progress nonetheless. I hugged her back and we remained coiled for what seemed like oblivion.

I had read somewhere that physical intimacy is the best method for a warring couple to make amends and my experience left me with no doubts about the theory. In fact I now have a little learning of my own to add – a heated argument is also one of the best possible aphrodisiacs for a couple. Our love making achieved levels of primitive desire, hunger and raw sensuality that had remained hidden from us till that day. We lay entangled with each other till the wee hours of the morning, pausing for breath before resuming our journey to ecstasy like a long distance train, chugging away on its destined path.

The next morning, we headed back as per plan. The atmosphere in the car was sullen and morose, each one engulfed in a sulky disappointment about the good times having come to an end. The

Punjabi band was not as loud as it had been; there were no jokes being cracked and no beer cans being passed around. Everyone seemed lost in their own world, staring into oblivion as I sat clutching Ayesha's hand with my mind racing away on a completely tangential path.

Before we left Agra, Varun had handed over a sheet of paper with a summary of the trip expenses to Abhay for being passed around. Including the room rent, fuel and other miscellaneous expenses the trip had cost us a whooping Rs 16,000 per head. A weekend trip to Agra, I had best pegged at Rs 3,000 – 4,000 per head and had even planned to chivalrously contribute on Ayesha's behalf and earn some brownie points in the bargain.

After my recent trip home, my bank balance had shot up to about Rs 10,000 which as per my estimate should have been enough for both of us. Little had I known that the room was costing us Rs 12,000 per night and the Coke bottles we had liberally used as mixers had each left us poorer by Rs 200. I had told Varun that I wasn't carrying enough cash and that I would hand over my share of the expenses to Ayesha the next day, but I couldn't figure out an avenue to raise the Rs 8,000 which I would be short of, despite wiping my bank account clean. *As for Ayesha, I guess she will have to foot her own bill this time round.*

Seven

The hostel, when I returned to it, was just not the same. Everything from its texture to its color seemed to have altered during my brief absence. It was suddenly a picture of gloom and despair; a world away from the reality that I had returned from, a reality where Ayesha and I were together. The sullenness of the surroundings was only compounded by the sight of an even gloomier Senti who was lying on his bed, staring at the ceiling – a breathing relic that had witnessed better times. “How is your aunt doing now?” he enquired, in a tone better suited for giving condolences.

No, I can’t ask him for the money. Given his mind frame, I wouldn’t want to tell him about my trip. And another lie… well, that is best avoided. Besides, I don’t think he will have the amount I require. Bengali, yes… he might come in handy. After dumping my bag and exchanging basic pleasantries with Senti, I set out on my search for Bengali *Baba.* After a brief hunt I was able to locate him at one of the basketball courts where he was busy giving tips and showing off his near absent basketball skills to a group of enthusiastic juniors. Evidently, he didn't much appreciate the intrusion and I had to literally tear him off his engagement.

"What is it? In case it missed your maggot infested eyes, I was teaching them some interesting tricks out there. This better be good," he said vocally expressing his exasperation. As I have already iterated in the past, Bengali is not the kinds to be trusted with a secret. When it came to holding one, he would even give news hungry scribes a run for their money. However, in dealing with Senti's issue he had exhibited a comforting degree of maturity and compassion. *He does tend to exhibit humanitarian tendencies when it comes to matters of the heart.* Eager to share the excitement of my exploits with any willing soul, I told him about my recent outing; all but some elementary details that he could do without.

"Impressive… very impressive. So, are you going to tell me all the interesting things you guys did, or am I supposed to let my imagination do the wild running around?" he responded with a cunning wink. "U damned pervert, nothing of that sort happened. Stop your imagination from making unnecessary efforts and instead make yourself useful. I need 8,000 rupees urgently. We overshot the trip budget and I need it for my part of the contribution. If you have some money that you can spare for about a month, please lend it to me," I came straight to the point.

"I will have some money for sure, some two or three thousand, not more. I guess you can take that and borrow the rest from someone else. And just for my information, where are you expecting to raise it in a month's time from?"

"Well, I will need to cook some story for my folks, haven't really thought about that as yet, but as of now I need to get over this immediate obstacle. Thanks for your offer, please check the exact amount that you can spare and let me know tomorrow morning and in the meantime I will try and figure out as to who else I can borrow the rest from. I just wish I am able to raise the money by tomorrow, else it will become a big embarrassment in front of Ayesha," my fears spilled out.

"I know what you mean. I wish I had the amount of money you needed. I mean, you are making us all proud by dating one of the hottest chicks in our class and there is nothing more that we can do to help. You know what I think; I think all the hostellers should have contributed for your trip," as he said these words, his expressions shifted from empathy to a thinking one. Something was churning within his mischief factory and when Bengali was thinking, one could only wait in anticipation for the words of wisdom to spill. "You know what, I have an idea. How much money you said you needed?" he enquired, briefly emerging from his thoughts.

"Eight thousand," I replied, wondering as to what possible idea could help me with my situation. "We can carry out a contribution drive in the hostel and if we are able to get 50 rupees each from some 160 guys, we are home," he summarized with an optimistic smile. I could not say that I shared the same degree of optimism though. "Nice thought, but my friend, not everyone is as generous a soul as your esteemed self. Why would people want to part with their money for funding my merrymaking? Besides, you don't expect me to share my personal affairs with the entire world, do you?"

"Well, I am suggesting nothing of that sort. Think out of the box my boy, think out of the box. If you were prepared to cook up a story to get the money from your folks, why can't we do that now?" he spoke with the air of a learned professor humoring one of his lesser gifted students. "Meaning?" I was still far from being clued on. "What if we tell people," he paused briefly, "well about some medical emergency that you need the money for?"

"No, that won't do. You can always call your parents if you need money for any such thing. It needs to be something believable, urgent and yet something that you can't be expected to turn to your parents for. Let me think," he corrected himself before I could interject and slipped back into the world of his thoughts only to emerge moments later.

"How about this; you were driving a car and hit a pedestrian who is now in hospital. You obviously do not have a driving license and unless you foot the hospital bill, they are threatening to involve the police. Your parents of course are not going to take kindly to you driving about without a license and bumping into unsuspecting amblers. That negates any possibility of approaching them to bail you out from the muddle. This could work."

Bengali's brain had once again lived up to its image and he had managed to spring out a possible solution to my ordeal out of thin air. The next fifteen minutes were spent in polishing out the story and adding some finer aspects to make it more believable and gripping. "It is important that we appeal to their sense of excitement, that will ensure healthy contributions," he had opined.

The pedestrian was a street urchin, a little girl who had decided to cross the road just when the lights had turned green. I was on my way to the blood bank to get the correct blood type for my aunt who was hospitalized and in the ensuing hurry; I had missed noticing the girl while suddenly accelerating. The urgent requirement of blood justified the act of driving my uncle's car instead of depending on public transport and since the family was already distraught, it also added credence to why they had been omitted from the entire episode as well.

The story had started to sound credible but for measures of safety we had decided to restrict our collection efforts to our juniors. Juniors would be more gullible to the story and involving our classmates or seniors would have meant a higher risk in the event that any unforeseen chink was spotted in the story. Bengali was proud of his little scheme and decided to lead its execution as well.

"I will do the talking and you sit there with a sullen face as though your world could come down crashing any minute," he instructed as we headed towards our first target, a dormitory in the first wing of the hostel that housed six class eighth students.

Two of the dormitory residents were missing and the remaining four heard Bengali's story intently. I sat there with a grim look, marveling at his oratorical abilities as he weaved together a heart wrenching story, leaving no doubts among his audience that unless they came forward and helped, I was going to spend the rest of my breathing years behind bars in a jail cell. They opened their wallets uninhibitedly and we collected a total of 640 rupees, an astounding average of 160 rupees per head. More importantly, all four volunteered to help with the collection and took up the task of collecting contributions from their juniors.

"What do you think now?" Bengali enquired with a triumphant look as we left the room. I could only bow and acknowledge his greatness.

Within the next hour, we had collected a total of 3000 rupees on our own and not to mention the fleet of about 12 volunteers who were wholeheartedly engaged in spreading our collection network to all possible nooks and corners of the hostel. A fellow hosteller in trouble and an engaging description of the incident was evoking sympathy of no mean order and as a result the contributions were pouring in unabashed. "Sorry to hear about your accident *Bhaia*. I had some XXX rupees that I have given to YYY (one of our collection volunteers)," some juniors who had heard the story walked up to me and stated. Whether they were expressing genuine sympathy or simply confirming if their money had gone for the right cause, one thing was certain that Bengali's plan had clicked a chord.

I had stationed myself in Bengali's room and before the night ended, the combined booty raised by our volunteers and the two of us stood at a staggering 11,280 rupees. The gesture of nearly all my hostel mates rising to stand by me in my hour of need was overwhelming and I could feel a remorseful burden of guilt knotting up somewhere between my throat and stomach. Though the rudimentary relief from having overcome the immediate obstacle was doing well to cloud the guilt, every time someone made a concerned remark I couldn't help but loathe at my greedy, profane self.

"Here, your 8,000 rupees. And stop looking like you have just robbed some poor man of his daily bread. The 100 odd rupees that people have contributed are not going to leave them any poorer," Bengali said, handing me the amount that we had originally sought out to raise.

"That's not the point. They gave this money thinking that I was in some sort of a trouble and it doesn't feel great to have swindled them in this manner. It just feels cheap ... and disgusting," I tried to reason with him fully aware that the time for any such arguments had well lapsed.

"But you were in a spot of trouble, weren't you? Just that your trouble was a kind that not many would understand and hence we tweaked it into one that people could relate to. They thought that they were contributing money for getting you out of trouble and that is exactly what they have done," he came to the rescue of my moral fiber which was on the brink of being shattered by the heinous act that we had inconsiderately carried out.

It was a weird tussle. I was feeling terrible about what I had done and the more I thought about it, the more I cursed myself. On the other hand there was the reprieve that came with the money and stood as a justification for my actions. A part of me wanted to shout and let everyone know that they had been taken for a ride and the reason for which they had contributed their money was purely fictional, while there was another part which was happy that my immediate crisis had been resolved. I was the referee and had to decide the fate of the tussle and I chose the easy way out – I opted to side with Bengali's wisdom.

"And what if they were to discover that the story was fabricated?" I argued, more from the need of convincing myself than enforcing my point of view. "If either of us goes about bragging, people will surely find out. Else, it is a secret between just the two of us and something that they don't know will not trouble them," he said subtly emphasizing on the need for complete secrecy. The thought was comforting. "And just so you feel better, the extra money that we have raised, we can use that for a small celebration in the hostel. *Holi* is anyways around the corner and what better time to make it up to them. Cheer up now," he added.

Holi, one of the most vibrant and colorful festivals, is said to have originated from an ancient rite of worshipping the full moon (*Roka*) performed by married women for the happiness and well being of their families.

Either the evil called examination was still awaiting its discovery or the *Gurukuls* followed a different academic session from the current day, but in all sincerity someone forgot to time the festival as per the convenience of its most ardent revelers – the community of students. Year after year the festival comes embedded within the dreaded period of final examinations, leaving a bunch of disgruntled students to make the discomforting allocation of their time between the festivities and books.

The already grim scenario only worsens when a better part of the preceding year has gone by in pursuing ones love interest and living up to the demands of a steamy relationship. I had not been on the best of terms with my books for as long as I could remember and it was becoming increasingly difficult to mend terms with them at the penultimate hour. They seemed to be adamant on avenging the treatment I had meted out to them by throwing at me all sorts of printed syllables which were nothing short of Greek, Roman or any other such incomprehensible language.

Ayesha was equally concerned about her preparation and though we continued to spend as much time possible with each other, we had decided to devote most of the after-school hours to studying. Our late night conversations had been reduced merely to one or two text messages being exchanged and mostly even these were used to communicate our frustrations due to the limited progress we were making on the preparation front. The times were trying and for a while I could not read a single page of the textbook without seeking a clarification or two, while my classmates seemed reasonably comfortable with the cryptic messaging and went on to discuss complex equations with the same ease as discussing a recently released movie. *I need to start attending classes more regularly. God, help me this year and I promise to make amends in the next one.*

"Hey, heard about your accident. Is the kid alright now?" Swati apprehended me as I was returning to the class after spending the break in the canteen with Ayesha. She had been her cantankerous best, a result of the anxiety caused by the looming examinations and it certainly was not easy for me to brush aside my own problems and give her the support she needed. I was drained. "Hey! Hi. Yes, all is well. How have you been?" I responded trying to fake interest in a conversation I barely wanted to have.

"I have been good. Heard about your problem and have been meaning to speak to you ever since. The kid was hurt bad?" she was clearly in no mood to let me off the hook easily.

"Yes, a couple of fractures, but she is alright now. I didn't see her trying to cross the road, so couldn't brake in time," I summarized the now well-rehearsed event for her benefit.

"Thank god that she has recovered. These things can be pretty tricky, you know. But, you were just about accelerating from the traffic signal, right? Then, how come the impact was so firm that she ended up breaking her bones?" she paused, looking at me with questioning eyes.

The meddling bitch - always poking her nose where it is least required. Wait! Does she suspect something about the story? Why on earth is she … well, interrogating me? Bengali? No, he couldn't have spilled anything. After all, it was his idea. He does tend to put rationality under the carpet when swayed by the need to boast and he does talk with her quite a bit. Is it possible that he might have said something that he shouldn't have?

Her casual quizzing had sparked off a series of guilt laden questions and I could feel an unknown fear impaling me to near numbness. I stood staring at her like a zombie and hoping that the conversation would not steer in the direction I feared. In the absence of any audible response, she decided to continue with her monologue, "You know, I had read somewhere that this has become a pretty common con now days. They deliberately jump in front of vehicles and act as if they are badly hurt, all to extract money from unsuspecting victims. Are you sure that the kid was actually hurt as much as you were told?"

My heart had skipped a beat at the mention of the word 'con', but when I heard Swati's theory I heaved a sigh of relief. She was only being her usual I-will-not-mind-my-own-business self and giving me a sympathetic spiel that I could very well do without. "Yes, I saw her at the hospital and she was indeed badly hurt. Anyways, if you will excuse me now, I think we might be getting late for the class," I brought the conversation to an abrupt halt and walked out on her without waiting for a reaction. *Phew, she can really scare the shit out of people. I need to ensure that I maintain safe distance from her.*

"20 liters of milk, rose petals, cashews," Bengali was reading out the shopping list he had scribbled on a piece of paper. *Holi* was only two days away and he had come up with a plan to spend the extra money that we had raised through our little scam. "We will prepare *Bhang* (Cannabis) in the hostel," he had announced. The consumption of *Bhang* is an integral part of *Holi* celebrations in various parts of the country and a few movie songs depicting the merry making of the actors under its influence had almost made it into a fashion statement. I had heard stories about its effect on people and was keen to experiment, but the only thing holding me back was the fact that our final examinations were to start three days after the festival.

I meekly voiced my reservations before giving in to the excitement of trying something new, unexplored and prohibited. Bengali, the ever resourceful, had somehow managed to procure the recipe of preparing *Thandhai*, a milk based drink spiked with *Bhang*, and we were now busy preparing the list of ingredients that we needed. Most constituents of the list were items of regular consumption that could be picked up from any grocery store. Bengali had also figured out a shop in the nearby market that clandestinely sold *Bhang*, taking care of the only tricky item on our list.

The shopping was carried out over the next couple of days. It was an effort to smuggle 20 cartons of milk inside the hostel, but Bengali was capable of smuggling in a live, fire-breathing dragon if he so desired. So, on the morning of *Holi*, while the other hostel mates were busy filling water balloons, digging mud pits and smearing oil on their bodies so that the colors would wash off easily, we were busy stirring two buckets of *Thandhai* in Bengali's room. Once the drink was ready, we dragged the buckets out to the common terrace and announced that the bar was open.

The drink tasted heavenly as the bitter taste of *Bhang* was well concealed behind the chunks of dry fruits, rose water and sugar that we had generously added to it. In no time, the news spread like wildfire and the terrace was flocked with enthusiastic boys of all shapes and sizes, waiting for their turn to dip the mugs, glasses, empty bottles or whatever else they were carrying into the buckets. The empty buckets were soon rolling on the floor amid a merry bunch of guys, some of them on the brink of rolling on the floor themselves.

The *Holi* celebrations in the hostel comprised of a bunch of hooligans smearing each other with colors, tearing each others clothes and finally jumping into the mud pit and erasing any visual semblance to mankind that remained. The girls of course were treated with more dignity and were spared the mud pit and the tearing of clothes. However, if rumors were to be believed, the situation within the confines of the girls' hostel was no better and there were as many torn clothes that emerged from the bins there as that of the boys hostel once the festivities ended. The chaos usually began right after breakfast and continued till the tired revelers retired to their rooms and resurfaced after a bath and change of clothing to feast on the delicacies that were served during the special lunch.

Feeling a little tipsy, we had decided to skip breakfast and straight away went downstairs to join the festivities, armed with colors and two bottles each of *Thandhai* that Bengali had the foresight to preserve. These were for those of our friends who had missed having the drink earlier and as able custodians, we were obviously entitled to a sip or two in the interim.

"Happy Holi," Swati surfaced from nowhere smearing my face with color concealed within her hands. "Happy Holi to you too," I replied, reaching out for my own packet of colors and applying them on her cheeks. "What's that you are carrying?" she pointed to the two bottles peeping out of my bulging pockets. *There she goes, poking her nose again.*

"Nothing! Just some *Doodh Badam* (a similar drink, minus the cannabis). Want to have some?" I obviously could not tell her about the actual contents of the bottle and a sadistic steak in me aided by my dwindling liking for her wanted to actually see her drink some of it.

"Here..," I offered. She unscrewed the bottle and took a couple of sips before handing it back, "Mmm... nice," she added. "Here, have some more," I said, shaking the bottle well before handing it back to her. The shaking of the bottle was to ensure that all the deposits at the bottom, including the *Bhang* would surface and find their way into her system. *If you do something, do it well.* "It tastes different, but nice. Thanks," she said before pursuing other targets for her colored hands.

Initially we thought that we had been duped and the *Bhang* was nowhere as potent as we had been told. We were all feeling a little giddy, but beyond that everything seemed rather normal. It was a little later that I felt as if I had slowly and smoothly been transported into a different world – the drink was living up to its promised intoxication. Everything around me seemed to be happening in slow motion and though I was very much a part of it all, I felt as if the surroundings were only a mirage that I was observing from a distance. My humor quotient also seemed to have shot up markedly and I was finding reasons to laugh at the most normal of incidents. I was not alone; the entire celebration scene had changed into one of senseless and lazy laughter. The *Bhang* had not let us down.

In a state of trance I took a shower, changed and followed the others to the mess for lunch. I can't recall exactly what I ate, but I would have eaten generously, for later when I was lying on my bed I could feel the tension within my stomach, stretching to contain all that it had been fed. I got up just in time for dinner to the tremors of an earthquake that I later realized was only Senti trying to wake me up. The dizziness persisted and as if bound by a magical spell, I followed my sober roommate right up to the dinner table. It was only a split second decision that made me take up a separate chair instead of surrendering my weight on his lap. *Swati, I need to see her. If she is half as intoxicated as I am, I am sure she will be a sight to see.*

Senti, who had refrained from consuming our potion, ensured that I came back to the room straight after dinner and hit the bed. It was only the next morning that my senses opened up to the world around me. Surprisingly I had complete recollection of all that had transpired over the past 24 hours. I had now been propelled to the midst of the reality that I had been comfortably witnessing from the ringside in my inebriated state. Thankfully it was a Saturday and the examinations did not start till Monday.

When I didn't see Swati in the hostel mess during breakfast as well as lunch, I started getting a little worried. *She hadn't had too much Bhang, but for a girl who was having it for the first time it could still have been too much to handle.* I was suddenly worried about her and hoped that my little joke had not landed her in any kind of trouble. Just then, I saw her roommate - Pooja, breaking away from a group of girls and heading towards the girls hostel.

"Hey Pooja, wait up," I called out, taking brisk strides towards her.

"Seen Swati somewhere? I have been looking for her since the morning," I asked, trying to sound normal. "She is sleeping. Anything important?" she replied, just as normally.

"No… well, actually yes. But why is she sleeping till now? I hope she is not unwell or something."

"I don't know she has been behaving a little weird since yesterday. She is sleeping continuously as if under the influence of drugs or something. She has not even been coming down for her meals and I have been sneaking food out of the mess for her," she said, signaling at the small packet that she was concealing beneath her *Chunni*.

It was surely the *Bhang*; and I was as much responsible as the drink for her current state. "You think she needs to see a doctor?" I casually enquired exhibiting only a measured degree of concern.

"I did suggest that to her but she refused. She is talking normally and doesn't have fever or anything. It is just that she gets up for a bit and goes off to sleep again. I am just a little worried because of the exams. I hope she gets over her sleep and manages to study a bit." I was feeling sorry for her and terrible about myself. True, I didn't like her much, but then I had given her the drink in pure jest and this was not what I had expected her to endure.

Later that evening, I made another attempt to patch up with my books but my thoughts again got in the way, only this time they were about Swati and the state that I had landed her in. *I hope she recovers soon. It's been a day and a half now; the effect would have worn out. She should be fine by dinner time. I think I should apologize to her; I will do that after dinner.*

As I entered the mess for dinner, I kept glancing towards the girls' tables to catch a glimpse of Swati and much to my respite, I soon spotted her. She looked a little pale and her eyes were puffy, but she was there – living, breathing and having her dinner. After quickly stuffing myself just enough for survival, I headed to the exit intending to wait for her so that I could apologize for all that she was made to endure because of my stupidity. I had barely stepped out from the mess when Alok surfaced in front of me. "Jaat, can I have a word with you?" he said.

"Yes, tell me," I responded. "Not here. Do you mind stepping to the side a bit?" he sounded annoyed. Not that I cared much about him or his annoyance, but there was something about his tone that made me follow him to the side, beyond an earshot of other diners exiting the mess.

"It was you who gave Swati the *Bhang*?" he enquired, his nostrils flaring. The question was least expected and as I mentally tried to assimilate the situation, I repeated a few of his words, "Swati… *Bhang*…"

"Yes, the *Bhang* that you and Bengali had prepared. It has to be one of you who gave it to her, I just need to know which one," he quizzed. I knew all about the *Bhang* and also who had given it to Swati, but he had no business going about policing people. His aggression was not only inexplicable but also annoying.

"Why on earth are you acting all flared up? Did Swati say something to you?" I tried to sound casual, controlling my reactions. "Stop screwing around and just tell me who was it? I need to know. It is about time someone taught you fuckers a thing or two about behaving with girls," he nearly barked.

"Oh yeah, and you are going to teach me that? She's too fucking frail to speak for herself or has someone appointed you her nanny? Let's just say I gave her the bhang. So show me what are you going to do?" his near threatening tone was too infuriating to command controlled reactions. I don't know if he was the first one to grab my collar or vice versa, but we were soon bundled up in a heap, exchanging blows. The loud invectives that we were pouring on each other were heard by others who chased the voices, curious about their origin, to discover us in our entangled state.

The fight was eventually stopped and neither of us spoke about its cause – I for the shame of the wrong I had done and he because fighting over a girl was considered as one of the lowliest acts in the unwritten code of the hostel. However, one positive that emerged out of his unwarranted aggression was that I was dissolved of the guilt I had been carrying about conning Swati into having the *Bhang. The bitch! Was only too happy to gulp down the 'Doodh Badam' and now she is going about complaining to people and sending them to confront me. I wish she would have stayed in her bed for eternity and never risen.*

It was only on Sunday that I was able to spend some notable time with my books and before I knew, I was sitting in the examination hall, scribbling away answers to the few questions I could decode. The seating arrangement had been revised again, and instead of Ayesha I was now sharing the desk with Charu, a girl who was infamous for her bestial belching and foul farts. My horrors had just about begun.

Eight

Like any walloping tide, our exams also had to pass and so they did. Ayesha despite her anxiety had put in substantial efforts, albeit in coming up with innovative methods for concealing her little chits. When we would sit together after the exam, she would continually dish out small pieces of paper from every conceivable nook on her being - from the folds in her socks to the belt buckle and shred them, only to be replaced by a new lot the next day. Despite the best possible tutor, I had not been able to muster the courage to experiment with such forms of academic assistance and instead was banking on the ancient method of studying to sail me through; of course, a few friendly whispers from here or there were always welcome.

"Hey, you passed in all the subjects, but I have a compartment in Physics..." she informed me when the results were eventually declared.

I had come back home for the brief break of 10 odd days that we had got before the new academic session commenced. "Oh, that's terrible," I remarked empathetically attempting to convey my emotions over the phone line which was incessantly buzzing with static.

"Not really. I would have cleared Physics too, had that son of a bitch not screwed me in practicals. Imagine, he gave me a 15 on forty... the bastard!! But thank god that I managed to clear Chemistry and Mathematics cleanly," she added with the grace of a fallen warrior. I had scored an aggregate of 63%, an all time low in my otherwise respectable academic career.

My father had never ceased to remind me about his expectations and this time round, as I approached 'the year that could make or break my career', he had only grown more assertive. This implied that my score and any visible reactions that might surface when I heard about the debacle had to be concealed from him at all possible costs.

So, while I went about eluding a false sense of confidence and determination about achieving my predetermined goals, I also understood the futility of it all. My career was going to define my worth in the times to come and I had been recklessly toying with it – a situation that could leave me in dire straights. The more confidence I exhibited for my fathers benefit, the more I cursed myself for landing up in the mess that I was in. The forced role play that I was engaging in was turning out to be an eye opener, erasing the mist that had blinded me from my target. *I need to be regular with my classes and concentrate on my studies. If and when it comes to that, Ayesha's parents will surely be more comfortable pledging her hand to someone who has a respectable career ahead as against someone who barely scraped through high school.* So, with a renewed resolve I returned to the hostel unmindful of the path that destiny had already charted out for me.

Swati was inking her arrival in the register at the main gate and as I waited for my turn, I was reminded of the unpleasant incident that had become fuzzy amidst all the frenzy in my life. Senti, who had called to share his own analysis of the year's results, had informed me that Swati had scored a whopping 88 percent marks, coming third in the class with a distinction in English and Mathematics – which included the paper she had appeared for right after the *Bhang* debacle. Though I had been momentarily relieved, I couldn't help but curse her for making a mountain out of a molehill. *I am sure she would have been studying in the comfort of her room, making her poor roommate bring her food while putting up a performance of being intoxicated - the conniving bitch.* Ignoring the brief glance she gave while handing me the pen, I scribbled my name and proceeded towards the hostel.

The hostel was buzzing with activity; old, known faces and new, scared ones, all carrying their belongings to their allocated rooms, sharing stories from their recent vacation or whispering in subdued voices. I was instantly transported back a year, to the day I had first set foot inside the hostel, escorted by an unwilling Alok to my room. *Alok, may his flesh rot and he rest, devoid of any kind of comfort.* The warden was attending to the boys and in some cases their parents, giving them the same rehearsed spiel about the hostel, reading out room numbers from a sheet in his hand and getting any old boy that he could lay his sight on to escort the new ones to their rooms. Everything was exactly as it had been except for the fact that I was no longer a stranger – I belonged here and the feeling was comforting.

Senti had arrived earlier that day and he walked up to me as soon as I entered the common area. "You are in room number 21," he said helping me with one of my bags. Having become the senior most occupants of the hostel, we were entitled to single rooms which meant that I would not be sharing the room with him any more. Noting the tinge of sorrow that laced his voice, I enquired about his room.

"Room number 24. Same floor," he replied, rationing the use of words in his speech. "That's great! It means I can continue to keep a close watch on you," I winked, trying to lighten up his mood. "So, how were the holidays?" I added for good measure.

"I am glad that you decided to come back. I had almost started to believe that someone had kidnapped you and married you off to some dung-cake making bride from the village. No calls, no nothing... How have you been?" Ayesha pounced on me as soon as I entered the school building.

We had spoken at least thrice over the past ten days but she clearly had been missing me. I gave her a slight peck on the cheek and walked hand in hand towards the classroom, muttering an explanation. "You know how it is at home. Mom is almost always around and then Dad had also decided to spend all his time lecturing me this time round. But I missed you like crazy." She acknowledged my sentiments with a slight squeeze of the hand.

The first few days, like in any new academic session, were devoid of much action providing us with enough time to spare for each other. We would sit in the canteen, on the benches adjoining the field, in empty classrooms and any other place that we could find - talking, holding hands or simply looking at each other. I had to continuously contain an urge to hold her or kiss her and in one heated moment I had even suggested a quick walk to the squash court, which she had sensibly declined. During school hours the campus was trampled by over 6000 pairs of curious feet and there was every chance that a pair or two could venture towards our point of vantage. Eventually when I could bring my brains to do the thinking it was clearly evident that the inherent risk in the proposition far outweighed the possible returns.

"But we could catch a movie or something one of these days," she suggested in lieu. The desire was not burning a hole only within me, we were both on fire; I was elated. As planned, on Friday after school we landed up at a multiplex in *Saket* and booked two corner seats for a movie that had been marred by disastrous reviews and hence negated the chances of a full house.

The selection worked and we found that our seats were reasonably secluded, with the next living organism - another young couple, seated after a gap of three rows from us. We cuddled up munching on popcorn, holding, feeling and exploring each other for the entire length of the movie. It was an exciting experience; the act of boldly expressing your love in the presence of an audience and yet within the permissible boundaries of decency was exhilarating. We came out of the movie hardly aware of its contents and yet feeling that maybe it should have lasted just a little while longer.

After an early dinner at a nearby restaurant, we reluctantly hailed an auto bringing yet another fabulous date to its conclusion. The composite nature of the community of A*uto Wallahs* and the fact that no outsider could tell one from the other negated the existence of our driver from the midst providing us with an opportunity to extend our date for a little while longer. We made the most of it by taking off where we had left, unmindful of the roaring traffic whizzing past us or the occasional glance that we could see the *Auto Wallah* stealing through his rear-view mirror. This extension too came to an abrupt halt when we reached Ayesha's colony and after dropping her home, a solitary but satisfied me took the same auto back to the hostel.

The next morning, I woke up with a severe stomach ache and a feeling as though all my energy had been sapped out of me. I struggled to get out of bed and had to literally drag myself to Senti's room, clutching my stomach with one hand and using the other to latch on to any kind of support I could find on the way. Senti was petrified at the sight I presented and made me lie down on his bed.

"Your forehead is simmering – you are running very high fever. We will have to go to the clinic," he noted. So, aided by two human clutches I was quickly shifted to the on-campus clinic. The doctor was summoned and while he arrived, the in-house nurse wasted no time in administering a selection of colorful pills and admitting me to the facility.

The medication helped in checking my fever in the interim but no matter how hard I tried, I could not summon any energy from within and resigned myself to a heady, trans-like sleep. The doctor ordered a host of tests collecting samples of various liquids and solids that ran in my body or emanated from it and enhanced my medication to near sedation. Over the next two days, I remained confined to my bed in the school clinic slipping in and out of sleep. Senti virtually spend his entire weekend by my bedside and Bengali visited a couple of times too. Among a host of other visitors, one name that came as a surprise was that of Swati. She came in briefly, looked at me, wished me a speedy recovery and left even before I could utter 'thanks'.

"Your *Bilirubin* count is extremely low," the doctor said continuing to scan through my report. *Well, whatever that means! Sounds like something to do with 'balls;' given my sapped self, I might as well be walking around with one short.* "Jaundice, it is Jaundice," he took a cue from my puzzled expressions and clarified. I had seen incidence of the disease around me and knew that it wasn't exactly fatal, but it did imply an extended period of complete immobility. Before I could fully digest the news, I had been efficiently packed and was on my way home. I could only manage to drop a text message for Ayesha, which she was likely to read only after she got home from school.

The doctor, vide a little scribble of the pen had confined me to the bed for full four weeks and I was not the only one constrained – I had been given a small list of items that I was permitted to eat, severely limiting the options open for my mother to pamper her unwell son. Fretting and fuming, she fed me *Khichdi* and other fluids that looked different but were similarly ineffective when it came to giving my taste buds any kind of exercise. The only thing that I was able to differentiate basis its taste was the horrible *Ayurvedic* concoction I was made to swallow three times a day. If any medicine could be effective in killing bacteria, fungi and other such undesired organisms residing in the human body, it had to be the one I was being fed. Thrice a day, the darned thing came so perilously close to claiming a 5 feet something human being that the frail microorganisms could hardly be given any odds for survival.

By the end of the first week I was nearly saturated with my television viewing and reading comics, when my father came to my rescue. "You are missing all your classes. If you are up to it, why don't you spend some time with your books," he said, clearly concerned; though more with my aversion to studying than my health. His suggestion, though devoid of any scope for negotiation, made sense considering that if I did recover within the stipulated time, I would be joining school with just a week to go for the first terminal examinations. *Just a couple of weeks more and I could have skipped the exams completely. These doctors, they can never bring about any good to anybody's life.*

Senti had been religiously calling me on a weekly basis to appraise me of all that I was missing – nothing significant, barring the few alien sounding topics that had been covered in class which I was now grappling with, without the aid of a qualified teacher. I had managed a couple of calls to Ayesha in the interim and her sporadic text messages kept me informed of her well being. It was a couple of days before I was to join the hostel that I got a call from Bengali.

"So, spoken to Ayesha lately?" he enquired after the exchange of basic pleasantries and checking on my health. The question did not sound spontaneous and his tone was wary too; I was alarmed. "We did speak a couple of times, but I haven't really heard from her for the past few days. Why? Is something wrong?"

"No, no… nothing wrong. Just that she hasn't been coming to school for the past few days, so was just wondering if she is keeping well. So, what all goodies are you getting for us?" his attempt at changing the topic was feeble and I didn't quite believe his explanation. But I had noticed the formidable form of my father lurking about in the background and hence could not put much pressure on him to start singing and had to accept his version without any debate.

The bitter medication lived up to the promise of 'more pain, more gain' and before long, I was up on my feet. Under the constant vigil of my father, I had also managed to unearth majority of the mysteries that were concealed within the pages of my text books. And as I embarked on the journey back to the hostel, I could not help but think about the brief telephonic conversation I had had with Bengali. *Was he actually implying something or is it just a figment of my imagination? But then, why hasn't Ayesha been responding to my messages for the past couple of days? Maybe she is unwell or maybe it is just a coincidence... Either ways, I shall discover soon.*

The first thing I did upon returning to the hostel was to inform Ayesha of my arrival through a text message. No response again. "Hey, has Ayesha been coming to school?" I checked with Senti.

"Well, don't think I have seen her over the past couple of days. Actually, I think the last I saw of her was on Friday. Why, all well between the two of you?" It was already the next Wednesday, which meant that she had not been attending classes for three days in a row now.

"Maybe she is unwell or something. I haven't been able to speak with her for the past couple of days so thought of checking with you," I replied dismissively. Although I had managed to evade Senti, my mind was restless and needed some answers urgently. Bengali! And thus I set out on yet another search for the only man who was likely to have the answers to the questions that were cramping up my stomach.

"Oh, welcome back. How are you feeling now?" he said, raising himself out of the bed with an effort. Thankfully he had decided to spend the evening in his room considerably reducing my efforts in tracing his whereabouts.

"I am fine. You tell me? And what were you telling me about Ayesha the other day?" I had learnt from experience that Bengali was most vulnerable to a surprise ambush and when it came to him, beating around the bush was never a recommended strategy.

"Nothing! I was only checking if you had heard from her since she had not come to school," his defensive deportment was a clear give away that he was attempting to conceal something.

"You called me on Monday and that was the first day that she missed school. You couldn't possibly have been missing her so much that her unannounced absence for just one day made you call me to enquire? She is not responding to my messages and I am really worried, so please come out with whatever you know. Please," I appealed to his benevolent side. A little more coaxing and Bengali slipped into a deep thought, his eyes looking at nothing in particular – his trademark pose before embarking on a discourse, only this time he actually seemed to be thinking.

"I thought she would have told you, therefore I had called to check on you," he eventually spoke before breaking into a thoughtful pause again.

"Told me what? Will you cut the bloody crap and get to the point? For God's sake," I was on the verge of losing my patience and he seemed to have mastered the art of making me do it. "Don't ask where I got this from," he said, walking up to his cupboard and dishing out a mobile phone. *When did he get one?* "Here, look at this," he said, handing over the instrument to me after pressing a few keys.

It was a badly shot video, possibly recorded on the same or any other similar instrument. Ayesha's face emerged on the screen. She was saying something, but the voice quality of the video did not permit comprehension. Suddenly another familiar face emerged on the screen; Manav, one of the day scholars from our class. A little hustle-bustle, adjustment of the camera focus and another image appeared on the screen, an image that left me cold and dry - the image of Ayesha lip-locked with Manav.

The camera that had been used for the recording was evidently held by Manav in his right hand. As the focus shifted again, I could see enough of the background to identify the location – it was the ledge at the top end of the staircase in the squash court. A numbing chill ran down my spine, preventing me from doing anything other than continuing to stare at the screen. As the images evolved to escalating levels of passion, I could feel spears of humiliation, horror, amazement and indignation puncturing my composure. A part of me refused to believe what my eyes were witnessing and the resultant tussle had entangled my thoughts into a dizzy mesh.

Suddenly, after what seemed like voices of protest, the video came to an abrupt end, jolting me back into reality. Bengali was looking at me, possibly searching for a cue to guide his own reactions.

"Ayesha?" I uttered dumbly. He nodded as I sat down on the bed, my shaky legs refusing to bear any more of the burden. I would have sat there for eternity, looking at nothing and thinking nothing, completely oblivious to the intermittent queries of concern from Bengali.

"Who all know about it?" I eventually spoke attempting to size up the magnitude of devastation. "I don't think many people have seen it yet. Manav had obviously recorded this without her knowledge and gone on to pass the clipping to a couple of his friends. It was by pure chance that I came across it and though I deleted the clip from the phone that I got it from, it is still available with Manav and maybe a couple of others. I had saved it with me so that I could show it to you," he explained.

Afire with a fierce, tearing pain that was tormenting me beyond endurance, I returned to my room. "What happened to you? Why are you looking as if you have just returned from a tête-à-tête with a ghost?" I had little control over my façade which was screaming foul and Senti was clearly worried.

"Nothing! Just feeling a little weak. I think I will sleep for a while," the excuse, though feeble, borrowed some credibility from my recent ill health and he reluctantly excused himself, leaving me to my own perils.

I spread myself on the bed trying to come to terms with the sordidness of the whole business, nursing a growing loathing for Ayesha for having done this to me and myself for having been blinded by her glamour. *I should have known. It was never meant to be, she and I are completely different individuals. But, I could never have imagined that she would be so desperate… I had no reasons to think on these lines. It was what, only about a month that I was away… and she couldn't control her urges even for that long? And what were all those promises, all the talk about having found the love of her life? Was all of it a farce? How could she have done this to me?*

Suddenly I would find myself transported back in time to one of our happy moments together and even before I could forge a smile, the frivolity of it all would be staring me in the face. I wanted to give her the benefit of doubt; I wanted to believe that her love was not a mere opportunistic drivel but a more meaningful reality, but my thoughts were overpowered by the disgust for what I had witnessed. *I should have known. It was just a time-pass affair for her and I was just an addition to the list of guys she had kissed. Ssshhh… How could I have been so blind to have missed it completely? I had been going about proclaiming the solidity of our love at the top of my voice, and now how would I face the same people after what she had done to me? What right did she have to reduce me into a pitiable target for ridicule? And all because I had truly loved her!*

I could not bring myself to eat the *chapattis* that Senti had smuggled for me and my thoughts would prohibit me from retiring into the arms of sleep. When a persisting line of thought would permit my eyes the luxury of feeling heavy, a completely new reflection would jar me to rapt attention. I was tired and exhausted, but I could not give up.

Like a soaring bird hit by a stray bullet, my love life had come crashing down, but I had to think of a way to redeem myself. Ayesha was not the end of the world, yet it had been a while that my world had comprised of anyone but her. Her brutality had not left any scope for our relationship to mend, but I also could not sit back like a mute spectator and watch the climax of my own story unfold. There had to be something I could do, something that would make me feel like a man again.

It was when the persistent ticking of the clock started to get interspersed with the early morning revelry of feathered beings that I forcibly brought my scattering thoughts to a standstill and got out of the bed. I had spent the whole night thinking and yet had failed to come up with anything conclusive to show for it. I was still as bewildered as I had been the previous evening with the only notably addition to my condition being the steady thumping I could feel within my head. Negotiating the severe headache, I took my time to get ready and despite missing breakfast, could only make it to school a few minutes after the first bell.

The classroom was scarcely populated with most students preferring to stay home and prepare for the examinations. Ayesha, among others, was conspicuous with her absence. Though I had not exactly expected to see her in class, but the reality was only another bitter pill that I had to swallow. And adding to my misery was Manav, who was parked in the last row, happily chatting away with his friends.

The teachers, having completed their syllabi were engaged in addressing problems that were being generously hurled at them by the more enthusiastic of the lot that had showed up in class. They were happy to ignore those who didn't have anything to clarify and I was happy to be left alone to drift into my own thoughts once again. My problems were far too complex than the ones being discussed and a simple trigonometric equation or a chemical formula would not be adequate to resolve them. By the time the bell announcing the break rang, I had outlined a fuzzy course of action and I walked towards Manav with an arduous determination. *Let's see how it goes. I don't think I know what I am doing, but something needs to be done.*

"Manav, I need to speak with you. Would you care to step out of the class?" I spoke, my disgust making the words sound more venomous than intended. "What is it? Tell me here," he replied looking a little worried and obviously preferring the comforting company of his friends.

"No, it is not something that can be discussed here. Don't worry, it wont take more than a couple of minutes," I replied, trying to sound a little less menacing. Halfheartedly he picked himself up and followed me out of the class.

"I have seen the recording. Yours and Ayesha's," I announced. "Oh… But where did you see it?" he was clearly not expecting me to know anything about it, a positive sign. *It means that the clip has not been circulated widely.* He obviously had not accounted for Bengali's resourcefulness and was shocked at the leak of what he had assumed to be a closely guarded secret. "That's not important. What is important is why did you do it?"

"Who on earth are you to tell me what to do and what not to? If you have any problems, why don't you speak with her? I didn't rape her or something, whatever happened, happened because she wanted it to happen," he lacked any signs of remorse; rather he seemed eager to confront me for having brought up the topic at all.

"I am not blaming you for what happened between you two. All I want to know is the reason for you to record it. What is it that you wanted to prove? Do you realize what this could mean for a girl and what if someone did that to your sister?" my repugnance was mounting with every passing second.

"Stop it. Don't you dare bring my sister into this, and if you are so worried about your sweetheart's image, why don't you ask her to keep her legs crossed instead of preaching to me," he said before mockingly adding, "and if you are feeling left out, I can lend you my little black book. It has a reasonably long list of horny bitches that you could try your luck on." From the corner of my eyes, I noticed a couple of his friends walking towards us in anticipation of something that needed their intervention. Undoubtedly they were aware of his escapade and he had added the last sentence to ridicule me in their presence.

I was simmering with rage. "You think you have one ball too many?" were my last words to him before landing a forceful kick between his legs. It was enough that he had made out with Ayesha and recorded it for the sake of some demented pleasure, but making a fool of me in front of others was beyond all tolerable limits. As if his lowly act was not enough, the bastard did not have a single ounce of remorse for what he had done. I was not feeling any sympathy for Ayesha, but I knew that she had been wronged and if standing up for her was the last act that I had to do for the sake of our love, I was prepared for it. I followed up the kick with a sock in the face, before his two friends caught me and pulled me away from him.

"Leave him… you bastards," I heard a scream followed by the sound of shoes running in the corridor. It was Senti and close on his heels was Bengali. Without waiting for an explanation, Senti pulled one of the guys to the ground while Bengali announced his entry by way of a punch that landed on the nose of the other guy who was holding me. Finding myself free from their clutches, I jumped back on a bleeding Manav with all my might. The commotion soon caught attention of the passersby and within a matter of minutes, there were a good dozen or more hostellers pounding away on the three 'enemies', unconcerned with the reason for the brawl.

For the ten odd minutes that the commotion lasted, the corridor outside our classroom resembled a wrestling stadium; a group of warriors displaying their brutal might, surrounded by a horde of curious onlookers glad to be sitting beyond the fence. The spectacle continued till Manav and his gang resigned to their fate and gave up any form of resistance. Like a guerilla battalion having managed a successful coup, the gang of hostellers receded leaving behind a terrified crowd and three bloody beings. No one asked me for any explanations as we headed towards the hostel mess for our afternoon tea.

As I exited the crime scene flanked by Senti and Bengali, I caught a glimpse of Alok detaching himself from the crowd of onlookers and joining our victorious gang on its retreat. I was too overwhelmed to notice. Like a family, my hostel mates had yet again stood by me in my time of need without even being bothered by the nuances of reason and logic. The victims were surely going to approach the authorities and there was going to be a reprimand, but what the heck – we would together figure out a way to handle that. The sight of a screaming Senti, running for my aid was relaying in front of my eyes again and again and had I not exhausted my tear reserves during the preceding night, I am not sure whether I would have succeeded in containing them.

Nine

The 'fight' was the center of most discussions within the hostel for days to follow. The unfortunate ones who had missed out on the exhibition were eager to hear about it and those who had managed to strike a blow or two were busy painting profusely blown up descriptions of their heroics. The reason why it had all started was inconspicuously absent from doing the rounds and all that mattered was that there were a bunch of day scholars trying to rough up a fellow hosteller. Appreciatively, most people refrained from approaching me for an explanation.

"What had happened there?" Senti was first to pop the question and he did that when we returned to our rooms later that day. I was still overwhelmed at the un-Senti-like emotions he had displayed earlier and the least I could do in turn was to tell him the truth. We sat in my room and I went on to narrate the entire episode, right from Ayesha's sudden disappearance, the MMS clip to my consequent confrontation with Manav. Speaking about it was not easy and I had to struggle with the initial bits, but eventually when I was done telling him, I felt relieved – as though an inexplicable burden I was carrying had been withdrawn.

"You did the right thing. It is not about Ayesha or any other girl for that matter. Someone had to tell the bastard that what he did was wrong and I am glad that you did it," he voiced his perspective before going on to give me a long lecture on how I should not let 'a mere girl' impact me so much and how I deserved someone much better. Though he was going about the discourse very seriously and with visible concern for me, I couldn't help but smile at the situational humor. Some of the sentences he was using were the same ones that I had used while counseling him after his heartbreak. *What goes round sure does come around.*

I had managed to vent out a lot of my feelings during the brawl and some during my discussions with Senti and this dual ejaculation had worked well for me. The sweeping and overbearing feeling of disgust had been reduced from being a continuous phenomenon to a periodic one and I no longer found myself languishing on the bed deprived of sleep. And when the sinking feeling did try to consume me, I had found an able distraction in the form of my books. I had taken to my printed friends with a vengeance, partly because I considered my fallout with academics a byproduct of my romance – a romance whose traces I had vowed to erase from my life.

Much to my amazement, Manav had not formally complained about the incident to the school authorities. Though some teachers would surely have heard about it, they continued with their façade of official indifference, not meaning to disturb the muck that was settling down on its own. Whether it was his fear of having to explain the cause or any other consideration that crept in his convoluted mind, I was glad to have been spared a reprimand. This act of his had earned Manav a slot marginally above the one I had originally placed him in – one reserved for the lowliest and most loathsome human beings. Now Ayesha was the only occupant of that slot, lonely even within the confines of my thoughts.

"Hey, how have you been? This fellow Manav, he must have really done something extremely terrible to have upset you so much?" Swati was the second person to enquire about the reason for the fight. I was heading towards the classroom on the first day of the exam when she stealthily appeared from nowhere and surprised me with her question. *What an occasion she has chosen to reinitiate conversation with me. I am sure the nosey bitch within her will not allow her to rest in peace till she discovers the real reason for the fight. Well, better luck next time.*

"Yes, he had," I curtly replied before briskly walking away from her. *Is she too dumb to take a simple hint?*

I entered the classroom, cursing Swati under my breath when my attention was suddenly wrenched away. There she was; Ayesha, sitting on her seat and hurriedly folding and stashing away little chits of paper. The worst thing about being happy in a place is that when things go wrong, there are too many ghosts about, bringing back painful memories from happier times. She stole a quick glance towards me before returning to her engagement, an arrogant dismissal of all that had transpired within the last fortnight. A little sound that was half a sigh, half an oath escaped me as I walked towards my own seat. The glance was enough to tell me that she knew that I knew and yet her careless abandon had flared me up with an impotent rage of dire proportions.

I was tempted to walk across and confront her; bombard her with the unanswered questions that I had been struggling with and bestow upon her the choicest of words and expletives that I had used to explain her actions to myself. It required no mean restraint, but I controlled my urges. The whole point of the socialized human being was to not give in to this sort of an impulse, regardless of how cantankerously the opponent behaved. *Let her be. You have an examination to write.*

Ayesha's indifference continued for the rest of the examinations, quashing any secret hopes that I might have been nurturing of a realization dawning upon her resulting in an apology or even an acknowledgement of her mistake. She continued unabated with her life, denying any reprieve to my wrecked ego or support to my dwindling esteem. By the time the exams ended, I was glad to be heading home; away from Ayesha, her memories, the squash court and anything else that could remind me of my first brush with love. I was not an escapist, but a momentary getaway I desperately needed.

The long summer break was a re-discovery of sorts. I cherished every minute spent in the company of my parents and relished every shower of affection that came my way. I had suddenly woken up to the selfless nature of their love and with it came a feeling of deprivation that made me want to soak up as much of it as I could. Like a thirsty desert traveler who cannot stop himself from drinking water even after his thirst is quenched, I was reveling in my oasis laughing at myself for running after a mirage in its lieu. So much so that I found myself enjoying even my father's words of wisdom and motivational speeches to ensure that I remained on track for my destined goal – an engineering degree.

Though I thought I had successfully relegated Ayesha to some remote attic in my memory, she continued to resurface and hound me every once in a while. I was heartbroken and my ego had been shattered. However, with each passing day I felt as though I could control her entry and exit from my thoughts. I seemed to be growing up, a year a day, and by the end of my break I was a completely different human being. I had not forgiven her but I understood her defiance; I understood that she was still suffering at the hands of her mistake and could not inflict more pain upon herself by acknowledging it. I understood that the only truth was that we were two very different individuals who were simply not meant to be with each other.

Love had attained a completely new meaning for me and I was no longer sure if I had ever loved her. I was attracted to her for sure, but love; I couldn't tell. I knew that the pain I felt was not as much for losing her as for the manner in which I lost her. Had it not been for this incident and instead, if for some reason I had been the one to initiate the breakup, would I be just as devastated? I didn't know; maybe and maybe not. I knew that the best way for me to overcome the pain was to let go; to excuse her as a meaningless distraction and instead focus on the larger purpose of my life.

I do not know if the transformation had come about because of the change of surroundings or because my parents had more than compensated for the void that Ayesha's love had left behind, but when I left home I had turned into a more responsible man. I knew that I had to make up for the time I had lost and make good my stay in the hostel by realizing my fathers dream. I knew that books were my best friends and any conscious attempt at forging a romantic relationship was at best frivolous. 'You deserve better and true love shall find you when it has to,' I remembered the words that I had used while counseling Senti and had later given him the opportunity to use them back on me.

The hostel seemed very different from what it had been before the vacation. It had not changed physically and its inhabitants remained the same, yet it seemed to have sobered down drastically. It was no longer a mad house packed with crazy characters but a necessary exile that had to be endured for the sake of ones career. I had started attending all my classes, doing my homework assignments and following as many of the rules as I realistically could. No, I had not become a geek. I still found time for the after dinner strolls, for playful banter and silly pranks; it was as if I had found a balance that had eluded me all this while.

I saw Ayesha and Manav and Alok and Swati, going about their daily lives in the most natural fashion and I was glad to be unperturbed. I had moved on and held no grudges against anyone, except maybe for Ayesha. And that too had subsided from the heartfelt loathing and contempt I had once felt for her to a sense of fury at having been wronged – something that I could live with.

"500 rupees, all inclusive," Bengali came to my room, seeking my contribution. Teachers Day was round the corner and as is the tradition in most schools, the senior most students were to take on the role of teachers for that one day. We had been given a timetable, indicating the classrooms that we were supposed to man for each of the periods in the day. We were also permitted to wear clothes outside the uniform, as long as they were formal. It was a big day for all class 12th students and a fair deal of effort went behind the preparations, right from deciding ones attire to the planning of the unofficial party that was held outside the school campus every year.

Volunteers had been grouped into several committees and their respective tasks had been delegated. While Senti and I had decided not to volunteer, Bengali was a part of the core committee that was in-charge of collecting the funds for the party. The individual contributions from all those who wished to attend had been pegged at 500 rupees and collecting my contribution was the primary purpose of this visit of his. I would have discounted the plea as another one of his schemes, but since I was better informed, I dished out the amount without raising a brow.

The party had been arranged at its usual venue, a banquet hall in the *Lajpat Nagar* area and barring a few non-adventurous ones was to be attended by our entire batch of 300 odd. There was a live DJ, drinks and food – all necessary ingredients for a fun filled evening and if the built up was anything to go by, it was sure to be a smashing hit.

The day went in the jest of dressing up as teachers and enacting our own interpretation of their roles - playing games, organizing talent hunts and general frolic with the students from the respective classes that we had been assigned to. The time table was followed but only for the first couple of periods, post which the entire school got transformed into one big amusement center. The almost desolate classrooms became a contrast to the buzz that had descended on every other nook and corner of the campus. The corridors, the canteen and the field - the entire campus was a picture of fun and frolic. While the girls looking pretty in their *Saris* and *Punjabi Suits* were busy exchanging notes on beautification and accessories, the boys seemed to be following them all around, flattering them with well meaning compliments.

Once the dismissal bell announced the conclusion of the official festivities, we retreated to the hostel to get ready for the unofficial continuation party. At about 5.30 pm, all the hostellers from our batch assembled outside the gate, ready to attend the party. Every individual had made considerable efforts in getting ready for the evening and even Swati was looking pretty in her black figure-hugging dress. While Bengali had put on a casual jacket to go with his denims, Senti had settled for casual khakis and a golf t-shirt. I was wearing a waist-coat to accessorize my casual attire of denims and a check shirt. The school had spared a bus to ferry us to the venue and once all heads were accounted for, we started, singing and laughing and shouting slogans to retain the tempo till we reached our destination.

Our destination, the banquet hall was barely a 15-minute drive from the school. It was a small building that comprised of one big hall and a small open area behind it. The hall had been converted to a large dance floor with disco lights and blaring music. The bar and food counters had been set up right outside the door that connected the hall to the open area and the extreme rear of the compound was made up by the series of restroom doors that lined the boundary wall. At the onset, the place looked a little cramped for 300 people, but given the shoestring budget it was the best that could be managed and moreover the venue was no stranger to such gatherings.

We reached the spot at half past six and most of us made a beeline for the bar counter. The crowd was scarce as most of the day scholars were still trickling in, driving down from various parts of Delhi in their fancy cars. After a couple of drinks and a confirmation that I had enough alcohol flowing with the blood in my veins to make me dance to the tune of the music, I headed for the floor.

The scene inside the hall was that of a mega sized *Punjabi* wedding with groups of people imitating every conceivable action from wiping their bodies with imaginary towels to flying a kite and passing it off as an acceptable form of dance. Bengali, who had entered the hall alongside me, tugged me towards one of the groups which had taken the form of a train – a human chain with the lead man chugging away like an engine and others following him like obedient bogeys. We joined the chain only to find that it kept growing longer in size with people from other groups breaking away to join us. Before long, most occupants of the dance floor were clinging on to the train which was swerving and steering and going round in a large circle on imaginary tracks covering the entire length and breadth of the room.

The train soon reached its critical mass and like any other vehicle being steered by a bunch of drunkards, it dissipated once again into the smaller groups that had come together for its formation. Even Senti, usually a nondrinker had permitted himself to indulge in some beer and Bengali had ensured that the indulgence continued till he broke all barriers of normalcy. Senti was entertaining us with a performance of what would qualify for a terrible mix of *Bhangra* and *Garba* with some *Kathak* thrown in, unmindful of the number by *Queen* that was blaring away from the speakers when suddenly the music stopped and the lights came on. "*Kaun hai behen@@##,*" he voiced his disapproval of the interruption by slurring away the choicest of Hindi invectives, craning his neck towards the hall entrance to identify its cause.

The interruption had been caused by Manav who was standing near the entrance, his hand still resting on the electricity switch as he surveyed the hall. "Where have you bloody hostellers vanished now? If you have the balls, come out and show your ugly faces," he screamed at the top of his voice. It was when I saw the people standing next to him that I realized the origin of his newfound bravery. Near the hall entrance, stood a group of 8 to 10 muscular beings menacingly staring at the crowd. They looked like the folks who move around with any respectable villain in a *Bollywood* movie and I could swear that I had seen one of them brandishing a shiny and sharp looking object.

In an instant all effect of the alcohol evaporated and I started to contemplate the moves available for me to make. The crowd was now at its peak and it was the sea of people between us that had prevented Manav from spotting me till now. But it was only a matter of time. I could feel my limbs trembling. It was one thing to go about socking people your own age and built and completely another when it came to a face-off with giants who looked like descends from a different planet altogether.

Just as Manav moved further inside the hall flanked by his friends, paid or otherwise, a near stampede broke out. It seems others had also realized the gravity of the situation and though no one was in a similar spot as me, they were certainly not willing to be party to whatever was set to transpire in that room. So while some people rushed towards the entrance cum exit, others headed for the only other door – the one that led to the opening behind the hall. You could hear people yelling and screaming with a sense of pain and fear and as if that was not enough, the lights suddenly went out propelling the hall into pitch darkness. By mistake or design, but someone had tripped the electricity switch on his way out.

The decibel levels suddenly shot through the roof with shrieks and screams breaking all barriers of rationality and amid the commotion that followed, I found myself exiting the hall from the rear door. There were people around me, but I couldn't tell who they were and I was too scared to speak for the fear of identification. The darkness had been god-sent and if I was to have any shot at survival, it had to be now. My instincts took over and I began looking around for a friendly section of the boundary that could make good my escape. I had barely begun my survey when the lights came back on, putting a momentary freeze on all my senses. Since a lot of people had managed to exit the venue, the crowd was no longer sufficient to provide cover and I felt like a living bait – exposed and waiting for the predators to arrive.

As a last ditch effort I looked around for anything that could be of help, perhaps a rod that I could arm myself with, when I noticed one of the restroom doors next to me. There was no time to think and on an impulse I pulled open the door and jumped inside for cover. The inside of the restroom was a familiar and comforting dark and as soon as I entered, I heard the latch on the outside of the door being bolted. Possibly some friendly soul had assumed that I would be safer locked from the outside. But I wasn't planning to venture out for a stroll anytime soon anyway.

Terrified to my bones I kept standing, my ears latched against the door and my mind conjuring up all sorts of scary images. I was worried that the loud thumping of my heart or the sound of my breath would give me away and I tried unsuccessfully to contain them. The community hall was not exactly known for its housekeeping and my nostrils were revolting against the stench and foul odor that was emanating from everything around. And yet, under my labored breath I prayed against being discovered, happy to bear the stench for eternity if required. The inconvenience was dwarfed by the hysterical horror that was making me tremble under my skin.

The commotion which was sounding distant earlier had moved much closer and all of a sudden I heard the door of the adjacent restroom crash open with a thud. Someone had kicked it hard. My heart skipped a beat. They were checking the restrooms. For that one moment that I waited for the next kick to land on my door, my entire life flashed in front of my eyes.

"This one is locked," I heard a voice as a step went away from my door and kicked the next one. It was not over, they were still around, but I felt a tear of joy trickle down my cheek.

I don't know for how long I stayed within the confines of the restroom with my eyes shut in prayers. It could have been an hour, two hours or even more. The noises coming from outside had long ceased and I had resigned to spending the night in my hideout. The stench was still around, but it was no longer tearing through my senses. Perhaps this is what they refer to as acclimatization.

Locking the door from outside had saved my life, but I only hoped that my savior remembered his or her gracious act and came back for me the next morning. I had just about started to size up the dirty floor for its ability to serve as a bed for the night when the latch on the outside moved with a slight creak. I once again became a living statue, the air within my lungs detained and my heart thumping away like drumbeats.

"Atul, it is me," I heard a faint whisper. The voice was feminine so it couldn't be Manav or one of his goons. Plus, she had called me by my name which meant that she knew I was inside. *It has to be the person who had bolted the door… I seem to be reasoning rationally; maybe all is not lost yet.* I let out a sigh, releasing the air from its captivity and slowly unlocked the door from inside. Someone pushed it open gently and I stepped out. It took a few seconds for my vision to adjust to the light and it was then that I saw my savior – it was Swati.

"Take off your waist coat. They might still be around in this area and this will be a dead give away," she ordered. She was obviously thinking straighter than I was, so I meekly obeyed.

"Did they get hold of anyone?" I enquired as she slid the waistcoat in her purse. "No. Everyone managed to get away. Someone said that the police were coming so Manav hastily retreated from here but I heard him ask one of his cronies to call him if he spotted you somewhere. I think they know that you haven't managed to escape yet and are holed up somewhere around."

"Here, when we step out, lean on me as though you are too drunk to walk straight. If they are not stationed really close to the exit, it might just work," she commanded as we stepped out from the banquet hall. There was no trace of Manav or his goons, but we chose to avoid the main road and took the arterial road inside the colony instead. Scared of doing something wrong, I continued with my staggered walk, leaning on to her for support for over half a mile.

"I think you can walk on your own now," she finally smiled, letting go of me. I smiled back.

"Well, don't stand there looking dumb. We need to figure out a way to get back to the hostel and there is every chance that they are keeping a look out on the main roads," she added, her smile consumed by a worried look.

"Why don't we ask him to drop us," I replied signaling at the manual rickshaw that was parked on the road side. "Yes, this might work," she said walking up to the rickshaw puller who was busy puffing away on his *Bidi.*

The man agreed to take us to the school campus in exchange for an astronomical sum of money, but we were in no position to bargain. Though a little slower than we would have liked, the rickshaw offered a distinct advantage over other forms of transport. Since manual rickshaws were not allowed on the main roads of South Delhi, we would be taking the interior roads to our destination – a much safer alternative given the circumstances.

It was way past midnight and the city streets were nearly deserted except for the one off vehicle that zipped past us every now and then. It was a full moon night and a pleasant breeze was adding to the experience.

"Why did you do it? I mean, you risked your own life to save me, why?" once I felt all my bearings in place, I sought a clarification for the one puzzle that had been troubling me since I had recognized her outside the restroom.

"You never understood, did you?" she replied with a mysterious look on her face. I had a feeling I knew what she was talking about, but I couldn't be sure. *Is she hinting... no, I am reading too much into things. Maybe I am not thinking all that straight after all.*

"What didn't I understand?" I took the easy way out – act dumb and ignorant. I had barely pulled myself out of the inflictions of a turbulent love life when it had come back to haunt me with this near death experience. If there was anything I was not looking for at this point in time, it was another romantic liaison. *She did risk herself for my sake, but I don't quite feel that way about her.*

"Forget it," she shrugged and after a brief pause continued, "I mean, I always thought you were a nice guy with a sensible head on your shoulder and I wanted us to be good friends. I tried to be there for you, but I guess you were too engrossed in your own world to notice."

"No, nothing of that sort. We are good friends," I opted for carefree abandon as the chosen line of defense, but Swati was relentless. Her well weighed words had an aura of truthfulness and she expected the same in return. The cycle rickshaw was making steady progress on streets that I didn't recognize. The rhythmic sound of the paddle, the swaying body of the puller as he strained his muscles to maintain momentum and the cacophony of shadows that we were casting while crossing varied sources of illumination made the situation into one grand opera.

"*Bhaia,* how much longer?" I made an attempt to break the monotony. "We are still in Lajpat Nagar … there is a fair bit to go. Should take another … half an hour," he seemed glad to be acknowledged and answered in broken sentences glancing at me over his shoulders. The interruption had not helped and I could feel Swati's unfaltering gaze affixed on me.

"I don't know. If you really must know… there were times that I felt you were intruding into my personal space; interfering when I wanted to be left alone and maybe that is what resulted in some sort of a barrier between us." She wanted the truth and though I was not exactly in the mood for a somber discussion, I thought I owed her the truth. She seemed to have anticipated my response and instead of a flinch, she reacted with a smile. "Well… tell me something, have you ever seen me interfere in the lives of Senti or Bengali or any of your other friends?"

It was one of those questions which are meant to have only one correct answer. Her tone did not leave any scope for me to think and I concurred with a slight sideway shake of the head.

"I have seen a lot of people come into the hostel and get colored by its ways only to leave as disillusioned and confused beings laden with vices. I didn't want you to suffer a similar fate and whenever I saw you heading in an off beam direction, I felt that I should warn you. Isn't that what friends are supposed to do?"

She had a justification even for being a nosey bitch and to my amazement it made plenty of sense too. She had decided to use our ride together to sort out the differences that had crept up between us and her perspective was now throwing a completely different light on the way I had been seeing things.

"And what about Alok? I agree, I might have carried the joke too far… but, you did know that it was only a gag. If you had problems, you should have spoken to me directly. Why did you have to complain to him and make him confront me?" It was turning into a game of sorts. She had a plausible explanation for everything and I was trying to put her in a spot by questioning actions that could not be attributed to the emotions of friendship.

"Alok? You are talking about the *bhang* drink, right? I never told him anything. In fact apart from a couple of girls in the hostel, I never even spoke about it. What business did he have to interfere? He spoke to you about it?" ironically, it was Alok's interference that had irked her but her surprise was indeed genuine. His source of information could have been anyone but her. "It did give me an uncontrollable high and I kept sleeping for god knows how many hours. I was angry with you for having played the prank just before the exams began, but why on earth would I go about complaining to Alok?"

Soon I had run short of issues that needed sorting and I felt much more comfortable in her company now. Her explanations seemed plausible, albeit to varying degrees, and I was left feeling like a moron at having misjudged her all along. The air had turned more jovial and even the rickshaw puller seemed to be humming away a melodious tune.

"You know, I think he likes you… that Alok," I said, more with the intent of pulling her leg than sharing the result of some complex analysis I had undertaken. "You think I am dumb? Of course I know that… but sadly he is not my type," she responded by pulling up her nose and shaking her head before breaking into a mysterious smile.

"*Saheb*, you would get down at this gate or the other one?" the rickshaw puller's voice brought our revelry to a grinding stop as he pulled up within a few meters of the school gate. We got down, paid him and started walking towards the hostel, talking and laughing cheerfully – a stark contrast to the situation that we had barely managed a successful escape from.

Ten

"Tomorrow, just when the break bell rings," announced Alok, just as I walked into the room. It was nearly 2.30 am and I had barely managed to change my clothes when one of the juniors had come looking for me. There was an important meeting underway at the dormitory and I was required to join in. Manav had sprung a surprise not only by planning retaliation but by breaking all rules of engagement and involving outsiders into an internal matter of the campus. My hostel mates had every right to be livid and the purpose of the meeting was a no-brainer; someone had dared to step beyond his shoes and had to be shown his rightful place.

The room was charged with emotions of fury, passion and latent aggression. It was like a war room with 20 odd senior students from class 11th and 12th, all rearing to let loose on the enemy. The heavy breathing, the reddened eyes and the somber expressions spoke of a fearful determination to avenge the attack on their unquestioned sovereignty.

"You managed to get away? We were all worried when you didn't show up and were planning to involve the police and go on a manhunt, but just then we learnt of your return. What happened?" Alok had stopped speaking as I entered the room and Bengali had taken over the baton, showering me with a flurry of questions.

I narrated the details, right from being holed up in a stinking toilet to the half an hour ride on a manual rickshaw that facilitated my escape. Any mention of Swati and her heroic role in the adventure, I deliberately skipped. I learnt that most of the other hostellers who were present at the party had managed to exploit the momentary darkness for their escape. A few who were left behind were not exactly under the spotlight and had made an inconspicuous exit once the lights came back on.

It was only when they returned to the hostel and took a head count did they realize that I was missing and that no one had actually seen me make an escape. The meeting had thus been summoned to decide on a contingency search plan and while the options were being debated, much to their relief, I had made an appearance in the hostel. Since the tempers were flaring, the relief had only been momentary and the agenda had quickly shifted to planning an apt revenge against Manav. His two closest aides from the school, who in all likelihood were passive participants in the coup, were also identified as eligible targets – when at war, it is only prudent to account for all possible allies of the enemy.

The three targets had been split among the occupants of the room, each one assigned to a group of 6 or 7 and a fairly simple plan had been agreed upon. As soon as the break bell rang, each member would approach his assigned target and start thrashing him without wasting time in any verbal exchanges. Like all decisions dictated by aching hearts, the consequences of this one too were left beyond the purview of discussions. A day scholar had dared to challenge the might and dominion of the hostel and an example had to be set at any cost. Any consequences thereof were of mere significance.

Alok, who had stirred himself clear of the original incident that had magnified into today's event seemed possessed by a wave of passion. He was clearly wounded deep within and restoration of the hostels pride seemed to be the only thing on his mind as he briefly summarized the plan once again for everybody's benefit. Yet again, the clannish fanaticism that the hostel commanded from its inmates had left me overwhelmed. I knew that the fervent reactions were larger than any individual and the emotions emanating within the room had nothing to do with my being at the center of the controversy. Yet, I felt responsible for the fiasco and indebted at the solidarity and passion that it had aroused. Once again, fighting my moist eyes from spilling any tears, I vowed my complete participation before retiring to my room.

The next morning, as I passed the corridor heading towards my class, I noticed a certain change in surroundings. The school building resembled a mini fortress with all the classrooms manned by the respective teachers and the corridors being monitored by the physical education and administrative staff members. The early morning frenzy was missing as all students were being sternly directed to their classrooms, not being permitted to hang about in the corridors. The situation resembled that of a city under curfew leaving no doubt in my mind that the school authorities had been apprised of the developments and had at last decided to spring into action.

"They know about it. All this *bandobast* is just to ensure that there is no retaliation from our side," observed Senti. He had been missing from the meeting last night, perhaps recovering from the effect of all the alcohol he had consumed at the party. But early today morning, he had appeared on my door seeking an update on all that he had missed.

"We must teach the bastards a lesson," he had concurred with the plan displaying a similar degree of passion as Alok and if the determined look on his face was any indication, he meant every word of what he had said. I gave him an understanding nod as we entered the classroom.

"Hey," Swati was waving at me, signaling towards the empty seat next to her. I waved back and walked towards her, scanning the room, looking for no one in particular. Manav was missing. As I eased myself on the seat next to her, I was glad that Alok had also not made it to class yet. I couldn't quite fathom the reason, but it was as if I was in the middle of some prohibited act and was scared of getting caught red handed. His display of emotions from the last night had overpowered any negativities that I might have been nurturing and I felt as though I was cheating on him by the mere act of sitting next to Swati.

"Why are you looking so serious? Didn't you manage any sleep last night?" she broke my line of thought. "I did manage a bit of sleep, but not before...," I went on to tell her about the meeting and the plan we intended to execute. As she intently listened to me, a worried look dawned upon her. "I don't know..," she had just started to speak when a peon from the Principal's office appeared on the scene and announced my name. I had been summoned by the Principal. The authorities had decided to stretch beyond the extra vigil and take complete control of the situation.

"What do you intend to tell him?" she enquired as I got up from my seat. The development had come as a surprise for me and I wasn't quite prepared for it.

"I don't know. He probably knows it all by now, so I guess I will stick to the facts," I replied honestly. "I don't think you should. It might get difficult for you to explain the reason behind it all. Plus, at some point this needs to end. Someone needs to make the first move and this might be your chance," she said with a near pleading look in her eyes. On my way to the Principal's office I tried to comprehend the meaning of what she had said, but in vain. *Never mind! Let me just tackle the situation as it develops.*

Manav was seated on the sofa in the waiting area with an elderly gentleman who could have been his father. He looked at me as the peon opened the door to the Principal's cabin and ushered me in.

"Good Morning sir. You wanted to see me?" I asked with an air of nonchalance. "Good Morning Atul. Have a seat," he acknowledged my greeting. This was the first time since my admission interview that I was in such close proximity of the man and he didn't seem anything like the ruthless being that my fellow students made him out to be. In fact he looked like a gentle fellow with eyes that reflected warmth and oodles of knowledge.

"I hear that there were some undesired developments at the off-campus party and that one of your classmates had called some people from outside to engage you in a fight," he spoke in a soft rhythm, as though reading out aloud from one of our textbooks. He paused to screen my reactions before continuing, "Your parents have left you here under our care and supervision. You would appreciate that such acts can not only prove detrimental for you personally but also tarnish the institutions image. We are all here to sort out any differences that might arise between students but taking matters to such a level will not be taken lightly. Please tell me the names of those involved and I assure you that the strictest possible action will be taken against them."

As I braced to answer the question, Manav's face flashed in front of my eyes. Sitting meekly on the sofa, he was a picture completely different from the rowdy and arrogant person he had been the last evening. I thought of his father, who like my own, had probably rested some of his failed dreams on his wayward son's shoulders. And I thought of Swati and the words she had spoken.

"I don't know sir. I wasn't feeling too well so I had returned to the hostel early from the party. I just saw Manav sitting outside, and if you are referring to the misunderstanding that had happened between me and him – that had happened within the school premises and quite some time back. I don't recall anything of the sort that you mentioned having occurred while I was there at the party."

The words had simply flowed, one following the other with a confidence that had taken me with a surprise as well. I didn't know who the Principal's source of information had been, but I knew that not many people could prove or even confirm my presence at the venue when the incident actually occurred. So, if Manav was to be punished and his father's dreams were to be shattered, it would not be because I had been a coward and decided to sing. His actions more than warranted the strictest possible action, maybe even expulsion from the school rolls, but I was not going to be an opportunist and account for his scalp when he was at his vulnerable best. I was a man of principles and that is what separated me from the likes of Manav.

As I emerged from the Principal's office my eyes once against locked with Manav's and I saw them brimming with hatred. In an instant the glory of my noble deed evaporated and as I traced my steps back to the classroom, I found myself questioning the superfluous heroism with which I had tackled the situation. *I should have nailed the bastard when I could. Lucky for me that he didn't succeed yesterday, but what stops him from trying again?* The teacher was halfway though the day's lesson and I quietly returned back to my seat, still not sure if I had done the right thing.

"All well?" Swati enquired in a whisper. "Yes," I whispered back. A little while later Manav also made an entry and receded to one of the vacant seats. *He has been allowed to come back to the class, so does that mean that they will let him go scot-free? The principal seemed to know exactly what had transpired at the party. His verdict couldn't have been entirely dependent on my testimony. So much so for the 'strictest possible action' he was harping about.*

I was busy cursing myself for my stupid behavior when the bell rang providing the teacher with the required cue to conclude the proceedings and make an exit. "So, what happened?" Swati shot out without wasting any time, as if she had been eagerly waiting for this moment since eternity. I was searching for the right words that could help in concealing my brainless act when I heard someone call out my name. It was Manav. He was standing next to me, his eyes no longer brimming with hatred.

"Atul, Thank you… And I am extremely sorry for everything. If ever I get a chance to repay you for what you have done, just let me know," he said with his eyes continually focused on the tip of his shoes.

He looked embarrassed and you can tell when a person means what he is saying. I was speechless. His apology was also heard by the other hostellers in my class and all of them looked equally puzzled by this sudden change of Manav's heart. The only person supporting a knowing smile was sitting next to me. Our plans for revenge had already suffered a blow at the hands of the school authorities and the extra vigil they were maintaining. Manav's unconditional apology came as the final death blow and through a flurry of communication to all its executioners, the plan was put to rest for the time being.

The tempers had settled as quickly as they had soared and school was once again back to being the educational institution it was always meant to be. The planning and plotting had made way for healthy academic discussions and we were once again bracing up to put our knowledge to test, only this time round the examinations were going to chart our destinies. With just over five months remaining for the board examinations, I found myself spending more and more time with my books. They in turn seemed to be reciprocating by displaying their contents in understandable English, possibly an ode to the significant amount of time I had spent flipping though them during the current academic session.

Ayesha's little secret had remained buried in the hearts of those who knew and though we shared the same classroom, her existence had fallen off my radar. I can't tell whether it was purely my imagination or a reality but she seemed to have mellowed down drastically and kept more or less to herself. The few times that I did look at her made me wonder as to why I had fallen head over heels for the girl. Her pretty face remained, but the aura of mystique that had pulled me towards her had vanished. She had been reduced to being just another pretty face in the crowd and if anything, I was glad that we had parted ways.

"Have you filled up the DCE form yet?" Swati checked with me during the day. I had permanently occupied the seat next to her and we had become the best of buddies off late. She would help me with my academic problems and counsel me when I felt low. The interference that had been a major irritant in the past was now something that I looked forward to. It was nice to know that there was someone who cared about you and was there by your side whenever you needed her.

"*Arey baba,* the form has just come out yesterday. There is enough time for me to fill it. I will get it done this Saturday. You have filled it already?"

"Errr… no. I was also planning to do it on Saturday only," she replied with a sheepish grin that made me burst out with laughter. She joined in.

Had it not been for her and Senti, I would have missed out on filling up forms for half the engineering entrance exams that I had planned to appear for. They were like walking notice boards who knew exactly when, which form had come out and what was its last date of submission and neither of them hesitated in repeatedly reminding me till I confirmed to them that I had managed yet another successful submission. There were others who seemed pretty serious about their careers too. Bengali for instance was busy filling up forms for everything from Hotel Management to Defense Services and Architecture to Fashion Designing. "The stream needs to recognize my talent and choose me, not the other way round," he responded to any query or suggestion pertaining to his focus on a particular career path.

Though cordiality had resurfaced within my relationship with Alok and we were back on talking terms, I never quite felt comfortable in his company. Though he hadn't exactly confided in me but I had heard rumors that he was working on going abroad for further studies. Since I had started sitting next to Swati, on a couple of occasions I had caught him stealing a glance or two in her direction. I would have thought that she was completely ignorant of the emotions he was containing within him for god knows how long, but her words came back as a reminder, 'You think I am dumb… he is not my type.' *Smart girl! I would be bored to death even at the thought of spending a day with him, let alone a lifetime.*

"This tweed jacket of yours, you think it will fit me? And if you don't intend to wear it, can I borrow it for the farewell?" Senti was in my room for one of our joint study sessions when my jacket had caught his fancy. With his innocent query a sudden harsh reality dawned upon me. My two years in the hostel were coming to an end. There would be no more Senti, no more Bengali, no more Kalu, no more Alok and no more the numerous other characters that had become an inseparable part of my life over the last two years.

I knew I would miss it all – the balcony where Senti had his first tryst with love, the squash court where Ayesha had introduced me to the forbidden pleasures of intimacy, the classrooms, the corridors and the canteen. Hell, I would even miss the dreaded morning P.T. sessions and the seldom palatable food from the hostel mess. The two years had transformed me into a completely different being and today if I found myself capable of surviving midst the uncertainties of the outside world, it was only thanks to the DHS hostel. A sweeping wave of nostalgia engulfed me as I started recounting the numerous memories, happy and sad, that I would carry along for the rest of my living years.

"What happened? If you are wearing the jacket, it is fine. I can make do with one of my own," Senti brought my quick trip down memory lane to a screeching halt.

"No, no! You can have it," I said, reaching out and giving him a hug. He sat dumbfounded, too shocked to react. "I was just thinking about how time flies. I will surely miss all the fabulous times we have spent together," I explained.

"I know, but this is not the end of the world. We shall meet again and share many more memorable moments," he responded with an understanding smile.

I didn't know then, but Senti's words had been almost prophetic.

We appeared for our board examinations and numerous other entrances that we had applied for before bidding a final heavy hearted farewell to the hostel. We had about a month before the results would start being declared and the arduous process of college admissions would begin. Both Senti and Bengali had favored my suggestion that we reconvene in Delhi at the end of the month and set up a make shift base to go about the admission process from a closer proximity to the action. Thus, when the board results were declared, the three of us found ourselves sharing a rented flat in *Mukherjee Nagar* near the North Campus of the Delhi University.

First to come were the board results and all three of us had fared respectably. Bengali had scored an aggregate of 86%, I had an unexpected 88% and Senti was the top scorer with 91% marks. We were thrilled and as a celebration of our joy, we picked up a bottle of dark rum on our way back to the flat. Senti had looked at the liquid alarmingly, tasted a couple of drops from his glass only to top it up with more cola – an exercise he had thankfully forgotten to repeat over his next drink or the one after that. Leaving an empty bottle rolling on the floor, we had retired to our respective beds, a content smile adorning our dilapidated faces.

The heady hangover of the next morning was like a signal for the times to come and the one good news was followed by a spate of bad ones. One after the other, the results of the engineering entrances came out and both Senti and I failed to even crawl close to the cut off percentiles. Bengali was suffering a similar fate as all possible streams failed to recognize his talents and left him to fend for his own. After the first few setbacks Senti had realigned his goals to pursuing Civil Services and Bengali remained unfazed as ever. I seemed to be the only one in the flat who was shitting bricks and trembling with fear at the thought of not getting into an engineering college.

Finally, Delhi University announced the dates for filling up college admission forms and having resigned to the inevitability of my fate, I joined my roommates in the act. We filled up forms for every possible college that existed anywhere within the limits of the city. This was the last ray of hope for us to garner any further education and we could not afford to leave even a single stone unturned.

Senti was the first to draw anchor when he enrolled for a B.A. course in one of the North Campus Colleges. Bengali had been a little selective with his choice of subjects and had to wait till the second cutoff list to procure admission in a renowned college for his English Honors course. I was waiting and hoping against hope for the third cutoff list to bring about some reprieve, but the fact was that I had no idea about what I wanted to do. My father was monitoring my progress with the eye of a hawk and I had managed to keep his hopes kindled with the names of the few engineering colleges who were yet to declare their results. But deep within I was certain that it was just a matter of time and sooner or later I would have to perform the dreaded task of informing my father about my failure.

I was at my lowliest best when I got the call from Swati which came as a new lease of life for me. ".... You should manage a seat by the third cutoff... no?" She had made it a habit to rescue me from the deepest of spots I managed to land myself in, and yet again she had done the same. I didn't have to wait that long and only after the second list, I happily got myself admitted into the B. Tech. course in Civil Engineering at the Delhi College of Engineering. The stop gap residence in *Mukherjee Nagar* would be serving us for a little longer than originally intended and more importantly, Bengali and Senti would remain my flat mates for the time being.

Today was my first day at the Engineering College and as I walked towards the nearby coffee shop, Swati in tow, I was nearly cringing with a nervous excitement. Instinctively I crossed the index and middle finger of my left hand into a makeshift cross and rolled my remaining fingers over to shield it from her view.

"So, what will you have?" I asked as soon as we occupied a table.

"You are in some sort of a hurry? Let someone come to take the order and I will decide what to have," she replied with her trademark smirk. I could not help but smile at the irony of the situation. For a better part of the time that we had known each other, I had been trying to run away from her and as destiny would have it, we were together sipping coffee yet again. The only significant difference being that I didn't want this moment to pass.

My subconscious was conjuring up images – of the Swati I had first met, wearing a white *Salwar Suit*; the Swati who with her interference had become my nemesis; Swati, the friend who had stood by me in my hour of need and the Swati from across the table, a picture of grace and vanity. It seemed as though the world beyond the confines of the hostel boundary had lifted an imaginary veil, exposing me to a completely uncharted dimension of our relationship. I could feel a strange tickling sensation in my belly and for the first time ever, I was falling short of words to say to her.

"We meet after a good three months and all you have got to offer is this dumb stare? Don't you have anything that can be put into words?" she joked. She seemed completely unfazed by the tension in the air that I was buckling under. *She knows. She has to know.* "So, you are planning to stay with your uncle only?" I made a lame attempt to shift the conversation to something that would not leave me gaping for words.

"I don't think so. It is a pain to commute all the way from there. I might take up a paying guest accommodation somewhere close by subsequently. But for now I will be staying with them only," she replied. We talked about the Delhi weather, the city's traffic, Bengali, Senti and a host of inconsequential matters – both of us inclined to skirt around the inevitable. "Heard that Alok has gone to Australia for further studies?" it was my accidental remark that finally led us to the zone that we had both been avoiding.

"I wouldn't know. I haven't heard from him since we left school," she said turning a shade serious.

"Well, I would have thought that even if you didn't, at least he would have made the effort to remain in touch with you," the tables had turned and it was now time for me to pull her leg.

"I knew he liked me and no doubt he was a nice guy, but I never thought of him as being anything beyond a friend. He proposed to me on the last day of school and when I declined, he got a little upset. He said a few things he shouldn't have said and that was the last conversation we ever had."

The stiff and uptight Alok, proposing to a girl was a difficult picture to paint. I was amazed at how the ever active grapevine of the hostel had missed out on this vital piece of information. At the same time, the manner in which Swati had mentioned the episode aroused a disturbing curiosity within me. "And what exactly did he say?" I quizzed.

"He said that I was making a big mistake by not accepting his proposal. He thought I was being foolish by running after a skirt chaser who did not value my feelings for him just like I was ignoring his feelings for me. He said that I would pay for my mistake," she elaborated.

"What exactly did he mean?" if was confused earlier, I was lost now.

"You tell me… You think I am making a mistake? Are you going to make me pay for choosing you over him?" the underlying meaning behind her questions took a while to sink in and when it did, I found my vocabulary failing me once again.

She sat there, looking at me with dreamy eyes and I had a very strong urge to embrace her. But instead I settled for a slight brace of the hand. "All I can say is that I will never let you feel that your decision was a mistake. Swati... I think I love you too."

I had run after love, found it and yet failed miserably. And now, love had found me, emerging from one of the most unexpected quarters and I had a feeling that it was here to stay.